Vasil Bykau

Alpine Ballad

Translated by Mikalai Khilo

Alpine Ballad

by Vasil Bykau

Translated by Mikalai Khilo
Edited by Jim Dingley

Book created by Max Mendor

Glagoslav Publications Ltd
88-90 Hatton Garden
EC1N 8PN London
United Kingdom

www.glagoslav.com

ISBN: 978-1-78437-944-5

Contents

Introduction

Vasil Bykau (1924-2003)

Vasil Bykau was undoubtedly the most significant Belarusian prose writer of the 20th century, who earned a wide international reputation through translations of his works into Russian, English and other languages. In 1980 he became a People's Writer of Belarus, despite having had his works considerably censored in the preceding decade. It was, however, a great disappointment to his friends in Belarus and abroad that he was not awarded the Nobel prize for literature in 2001, despite the support of such luminaries as Joseph Brodsky, Czesław Miłosz (both themselves laureates) and the distinguished writer and politician Václav Havel. It may be added that Bykau himself, a modest man, seemed least concerned by this event. The fact that in 1978 he was elected a People's Deputy of the BSSR, and in 1989 a People's Deputy of the USSR, witnesses to the high esteem in which he was held; nothing, however, was as powerful as an open letter in 1988 from the students of Navapolatsk (Novopolotsk) who described him as 'the conscience of the Belarusian nation'.

Born into a peasant family in the Vitsyebsk (Vitebsk) region of north-east Belarus, after his schooldays he studied sculpture at the celebrated Vitsyebsk Art School, whose distinguished alumni included Marc Chagall and Chaim Soutine, but was unable to continue for financial reasons. During World War II he served in an engineering battalion and from 1943 held the rank of a junior officer, and was twice wounded. It is precisely from the point of view of morally strong junior officers that most of his works are written. Recalled to the army after the war, Bykau began writing stories in 1951, and his first notable work was *Zhurauliny kryk*, (The Cry of the Crane, 1959) which is set in 1941 and depicts a small group of soldiers faced by a virtually impossible mission. Much of the novel's point of view is that of a young boy experiencing war for the first time. Already Bykau's concern with psychology and the behaviour of people in life-threatening situations is evident. In later works the themes of treachery (often by Stalinist officers) and the traces of the ruthless and cynical past in present-day Belarus also become prominent in his prose. Indeed, most of Bykau's intensely realistic work is based on his own experiences of the war, and has little in common with most heroic, panoramic Soviet war literature. Instead, many of his works analyse the wartime choices and tough moral decisions of young officers dealing with existential crises usually in tight spaces and over short intense periods; the decisions demanded are based on humanity and realism, often in contrast to the immoral behaviour of cynical commanding officers as well as to cowardice and treachery in all ranks.

After an illustrious career as a highly respected Soviet writer, some of whose works were too outspoken to be published in his own country, Bykau emigrated in 1998, four years after the accession of Belarus's current leader, first to Helsinki, then Frankfurt, and finally to Prague, returning to Minsk shortly before his death in 2003. After the collapse of the Soviet Union and particularly during his period of exile Bykau extended considerably the thematic range of his works, whilst retaining his strong interest in the Stalinist past and its present-day heritage of harshness and immorality. His prose written abroad became even more outspoken, and some of his later works took the symbolic rather than realistic form of parables, which illustrated obliquely his frequently bleak view of Belarus and Belarusians, although his concern for his countrymen's weakness and mistakes never obscures his deep love for his native land, evident throughout his works.

Before turning to *Alpine Ballad* (originally *Alpiyskaya balada*), it is worth mentioning three outstanding works already published in English translation: the first, *Sotnikau*, 1970 (The Ordeal, 1972), is a powerful depiction of bravery and cowardice, but without overt moral judgment, in which Bykau cleverly shows the strong temptation of self-preservation as well as the difficulty of living morally under Stalin. Narrated by each of the two partisans on a particularly difficult assignment in occupied Belarus, the ordeal is extreme and the mission doomed from the start, despite their being sheltered by some peasants, one of whom is the village headman, allowing further discussion of how to behave under an occupation as cruel as pre-war peacetime had been. The double point of view of the narration enables Bykau to achieve the high level of objectivity for which he was famous.

Another prominent novel, probably the most autobiographical of Bykau's works, *Myortvym ne balits'* (The Dead Feel No Pain), first appeared in a journal in 1964, but was subsequently banned for seventeen years, and only in 2009 appeared in full uncensored form, although it had been published abroad far earlier; its English translation came out in 2010. Bykau was persecuted by the highest political and literary authorities as well as the KGB for daring to write about individuals rather than epic struggles. The story is of a young officer who, detailed to escort some German prisoners in 1944, is severely punished because they escape, entirely through circumstances beyond his control. His disgust after the war at seeming to find one of his tormentors enjoying post-war life underlines not only the rigidity of Soviet views on World War II, but the longevity of Stalinist ideas and behaviour.

Finally should be mentioned a novel thought by many to be Bykau's best, *Znak byady*, 1982 (The Sign of Misfortune, 1990). In this work, set at the beginning of the war, there are no Soviet soldiers or partisans, only intermittently brutal occupying German soldiers and their willing Belarusian collaborators the *Politsai*. On a desolate farmstead an old couple face a particularly bleak future; the old man feels that only an accommodating attitude can save them, whilst his wife remains determined to take revenge. Particularly interesting are the extended flashbacks to the fanatical and ruthless dispossession of the kulaks (rich peasants) at the end of the 1920s witnessed by the old woman in her youth, for it is the bitter children of the dispossessed peasants who naturally join the Germans' local helpers. Any of the three novels mentioned above may be recommended to readers enthused by the novel now presented to the public.

Alpine Ballad, first published in 1964, is in some respects untypical of Bykau's writing, having elements of lyricism and intimate feelings not found elsewhere in his work. It is moreover not set in Belarus but in a foreign land, with finely detailed nature descriptions, and contains far more dialogue than this writer's characteristic terse exchanges and interior monologues. Following its appearance in Russian

(Bykau always translated his own works from Belarusian into Russian), the novel became popular and was soon turned into a film; the Russian version, incidentally, was considerably censored, and Bykau's original text modified, for instance, by watering down Ivan's criticism of the collective farms to Giulia, his naive Italian friend, as well as completely removing parallels between the Fascist and Soviet systems. Ivan frequently attempts to disabuse his companion of her idealised pre-conceptions, preferring honesty to beautiful lies and clearly remembering Stalin's appalling purges in the years leading up to the war, but towards the end of the book he recants and praises his homeland in order to console Giulia. The publication of Russian versions of Bykau's works often gave the censors, always suspicious of this uncompromising and relentlessly honest writer (of all the major writers of his generation Bykau never joined the Communist party), a second chance to change and remove anything that did not follow the Soviet version of the Great Patriotic War, their name for World War II (which for them, following the Molotov-Ribbentrop pact, lasted from 1941 to 1945).

Although *Alpine Ballad* is more romantic than most of Bykau's works, his qualities of taut realistic narration, honesty of principles and a strong sense of Belarusian patriotism are also evident here. In this, the only one of his works to give a major role to a foreigner, moral and other questions are mostly raised through dialogue rather than reflected in internal monologues. Ivan is almost the only character in Bykau's works to feel intimate emotions; also notable are the writer's experiments with a rather comic, though ostensibly realistic depiction of Giulia's speech. Bykau was known to his friends as a mild, modest man with a good sense of humour, although his prose is generally too severe and taut to allow any levity. *Alpine Ballad* was a new departure, allowing him, through the words of a foreign Communist, to show an idealized and completely unrealistic picture of the Soviet Union; it was Ivan's modest, though not unpatriotic, attempts to modify the Italian's extremely optimistic views that, amongst other things, fell foul of the censor.

This new translation of *Alpine Ballad* into English provides a welcome introduction to an early work of a major Belarusian writer acclaimed throughout the Slavic lands and beyond.

Arnold McMillin, emeritus professor
of Russian literature in the School of Slavonic
and East European Studies, University College London

1.

He stumbled over something, fell and immediately jumped back to his feet, feeling that he had better get away from this place, from the dead *Kommandoführer**, before the alarm was raised. He had to hole up somewhere, hide and maybe even fight his way out of the factory. However, almost nothing could be seen in the swirling clouds of dust that had filled the workshop, and he nearly stepped into the black crater created by the bomb. He ran around the hole to avoid snags in the dust, stretched out one hand, gripping his pistol with the other, rolled over a huge concrete slab that had apparently been ripped from the ground and hit something painfully with his shin. He immediately regretted the loss of his clogs when he jumped up barefoot and his skin began to burn on the crushed stone littering the ground.

Meanwhile, someone screamed behind him, and submachine gun fire rang out at the other end of the workshop. *Like hell,* he said to himself as he lightly jumped over an iron girder from the ruined ceiling and ran onto a precariously tilted partition. Although the dust from the explosion was slowly settling and clearing, it still provided good cover. He climbed to the very top of the partition and finally got a view of his surroundings. A gust of wind rushed

---

*	*Kommandoführer* – SS work detail commander in a concentration camp

over him and quickly drove away the dust. Using his arms for balance on his concrete perch, he reached the edge of the damaged area. The pockmarked wall of the outer fence was about three steps ahead, and beyond it, nestled in vegetation and quiet, without a care in the world, stood several houses, with a green forest just up the slope and the Alps—his hope, his life or death, his destiny—a stone's throw away. Taking a quick look around himself, Ivan stuck the butt of his pistol in his teeth and jumped. He gripped two of the sharp iron spikes that topped the fence and, without stopping, flung his body over to the other side. He did not jump immediately. Instead, he lowered his feet to soften the fall and then let go. He landed among weeds, grabbed the pistol with his hand and ran all out across the potato field along the tall wire fence.

People were shooting and shouting behind his back, and Alsatian dogs were barking somewhere in the distance. That was the worst-case scenario, but he had no time to think or change anything. Several bullets whined high over his head, and he felt that they had not been fired at him, that he had not yet been spotted. Tearing his bare toes, he climbed over the fence mesh and ran even faster along a slag path leading ever higher towards the nearby suburb.

The workshop blast had caused a stir in the town. Two boys were running as fast as they could toward the factory from some white house. Luckily, they did not notice him, and Ivan pressed on. All of a sudden, a girl in a floral skirt carrying a watering can stepped almost directly into his path from behind acacia shrubs. Her eyes widened with terror. She screamed and dropped the watering can onto the path with a clang. He rushed past her in silence and found himself on a wider street on the outskirts. Looking up and down the street and seeing no one, Ivan ran across it, scrambled through some thorny growth, and then fell. There were no more houses ahead, just a quiet unmown meadow on the hillside, with daisies dozing in its windless silence and wisps of grass gently swaying gently. The more distant gullies and ravines were covered with woods. The towering grey masses of the Alps in the hot June sky overlooked the landscape.

Stifling his violent gasps, Ivan stopped to listen. People were screaming and shooting behind him, the Alsatians were barking more loudly, but the sounds were coming from the factory, and no one seemed to be chasing after him. He ran the sleeve of his striped coat over his face to wipe streams of sweat from his brow, rose slightly, looking for a way across the meadow, and noticed a gully that came particularly close to the town. Fir trees, sparse at the edge of the woods, stretched over the steep slope down towards the gully. He jumped back to his feet.

With his legs extremely unresponsive and slack and his body growing heavier, the movement proved very difficult. Halfway up the slope he looked back again. The barking was getting closer, gunfire erupted nearby, but he did not hear any bullets—he was clearly not the target. Others were under fire. The pursuers were probably scattering. That made things easier for him, and he thought about the lads for the first time. And for the first time, his heart throbbed painfully. There were probably no survivors—the others must have paid with their lives for his freedom.

He was trudging uphill, wearied. The whole Austrian town was now in plain view behind his back. Its nearby half was covered with long hulking factory structures that resembled hangars and were dotted with gaping holes and bombed-out ruins. One section of the long fence was ruined, and twisted ceiling girders protruded next to it at the end of a building. The place was crawling with people. He hunched in the grass—a kneeling person could already hide behind the hill—and ran down towards the stream for several minutes. Screened by the hill, he finally straightened out. A wooded slope lay before him.

Ivan wiped his face with his sleeves and stopped running. Now he would make his way along the grassy gully. The terrain grew even steeper. Near him a stream was churning noisily among slippery stones. Ivan walked briskly until he reached the sparse fir trees. And then the barking behind him grew much louder. The dogs seemed to be very close, right behind the hill, and he resumed his exhausting uphill run. He only wished he could somehow get to the forest, to the dense fir trees, where it was easier to hide, trick the pursuers, or, if his freedom was forever lost, make his death count.

However, Ivan never made it to the forest.

He was climbing the grassy slope, strewn all over with scree, past large and small fragments of rock, and had almost reached the edge of a pine tree forest when dogs shot from behind the hill and burst into loud, furious barking. He dashed sideways to a small fir tree, bent slightly, and looked through the branches. Racing along his tracks over the hill, flashing its brown back in the grass was an Alsatian dog. Another Alsatian was barking hoarsely somewhere behind it. But the Germans were nowhere to be seen.

Ivan looked around and, realising that the thicket was too far away, moved his feet wider apart and tightened his grip on the pistol. Despite knowing that his survival depended on ammunition, he had no idea how many rounds his magazine held and no time to count them. He relaxed his muscles for a moment and tried to breathe more evenly. He had to calm down, pull himself together, and slow his heartbeat so as not to miss.

Meanwhile, the dog spotted him. Its barking grew more intense and vicious as it flew uphill, its paws pressed together, panting and wheezing. Ivan stooped behind the fir tree and pointed his pistol towards a sharp piece of grass-covered rock, judging that it was about fifty steps away.

The Alsatian was advancing in huge bounds, ears flat against its head, tail straight. He could now see its gaping mouth and its lolling tongue flanked by yellow canines. Ivan held his breath, trying to take aim as best he could, and fired just before the dog had reached the rock. He immediately realised that the shot had gone wide. The barrel of his pistol jerked upwards, the smell of gunpowder filled the air, and the Alsatian squealed with even more excitement. Hastily, and almost without aiming, he fired again, physically certain of the direction of the vicious attack.

And then he felt a glimmer of joy in his heart as the dog yelped, jumped wildly, flipped over, and crashed some twenty steps away, its body going into convulsions and spasms on the grass. He was about to dive into the woods when he saw one more dog. The huge animal with spots on its sides was powering uphill, stretching out its legs, breathing heavily. A long strap leash was dragging and bouncing behind it through the grass.

Alas, Ivan had not noticed the danger on time. He swung the pistol in its direction but never got a shot—the gun had probably jammed. He yanked his weapon back and slapped its bolt with his palm, but he was already within the reach of the hound, which gave a throaty growl and pounced. Ivan bent over and ducked behind a fir tree. The dog flew just above his shoulder, rolled over heavily and lunged at him, its jaws agape. Ivan threw up his arms, not knowing how to defend himself.

So powerful was the momentum of the jump that it swept Ivan off his feet, knocked the pistol from his hand and sent them both, the human and the animal, rolling on the ground. It looked like everything would soon be over, but Ivan managed at the last moment to grab the hound by the collar and push it back, making an almost superhuman effort to keep its teeth away. There was the sound of tearing cloth as the dog ripped at him with its claws. Holding the Alsatian's collar as tightly as he could, Ivan reached out with his left hand, grabbed the dog by a front leg and flung it over. They rolled over each other twice, and he ended up right beside the dog. Ivan spread out his legs and tried to straddle the animal, but it was coughing, wheezing, and clawing at him so furiously that he knew he would not last long. Gathering all his dexterity for the final, decisive attack, he spun on the ground, caught hold of the dog, threw it over his shoulder and fell on top, driving his knee as hard as he could into its ribs. The dog jerked, almost tearing the collar out of his hand, and yelped. Ivan felt something crack under his knee. The dog let out a piercing shriek, and the human pulled the collar tighter with raw fingers and pressed harder with his knee. However, the hound squealed, threw up its rear, pulled violently, and broke free.

With some brutal hardness in his heart, Ivan tensed in anticipation of another jump. However, the dog sprawled on the ground and lay there with its thick snout pointing forward, tongue hanging out. Its breath was rapid and tired as it watched the human with wild eyes. Ivan's right hand, the one that had held the collar, was on fire, a muscle in his forearm was twitching spasmodically from exertion, and his heart seemed about to jump out of his chest. For a few seconds, he also stood on his knees and shaky hands in the grass and stared at the dog as if he were some savage beast.

The human and the dog eyed each other wildly, wary that the adversary would pounce first. Ivan also feared that the Germans would appear at any moment, and those few seconds felt to him like eternity. He finally decided that the hound was unlikely to attack and cautiously rose to his feet. Never taking his fixed gaze off the dog, he jumped away and grabbed a stone from the grass. The hound arched its back and lashed the ground with its tail, but stopped short of a jump. The animal was probably no better off than the human, and all it could manage was a helpless whimper. When Ivan took a more decisive step backwards, the hound rose slightly and started forward, its leash moving in the grass. However, it did not run or pounce. This made Ivan even bolder, and he quickly moved up the slope, taking sideways steps toward the fir tree where his pistol lay.

The dog whined in helpless rage as it dragged its crippled hindquarters through the grass, crawled forward weakly and stopped. Meanwhile, the human snatched the Browning from the ground and started uphill along the gully, trying to make the best of his remaining energy to get to the fir trees.

2.

Five or so minutes later, he was already in the woods and running along the turbulent, clear stream. The forest floor was free of dead branches and trunks, but the numerous rock fragments littering the ground were getting in the way. Moreover, the terrain was getting steeper, and the climb was rapidly draining his energy. Afraid of a new pursuit, Ivan jumped into the stream at one point to hide his tracks from the Alsatians. The water sent a punch of icy coldness through his feet, burning his soles and forcing him back to the bank after some twenty steps. He climbed the rocky slope, pulled the bolt to reload the pistol, stooped to pick up a bent cartridge that had dropped on the stones, and suddenly froze. The babble of the brook behind him was now mixed with the sound of human voices. Leaving the cartridge behind, he rushed uphill, away from the stream, scrambled through the dense young fir trees and dropped to all fours, struggling to keep his breath under control.

His first impression was that everything was quiet except for the distant gurgling of the stream and the rustle of the treetops. A *Föhn*[*] wind was now blowing through them, and a disheveled corner of a storm cloud sailed into view from behind the mountains. Rain was imminent. Ivan cautiously

------

[*]   *Föhn* – dry, warm wind in the Alps

looked around and ran his eyes over the stones and fir trees far below, but there did not seem to be anyone else. He was about to get up to run when he heard a slightly muted but urgent voice behind his back.

"*Russo!*"*

Ivan pressed himself closer to the ground and lowered his head. No, that was probably some *Häftling***, not a German. However, why should he bother to wait for anyone, as if he were not in enough trouble already? He knew from personal experience how difficult it would be to make his own escape. It looked like the Germans had already raised the alarm, and it would not be that easy to get away.

He ran as fast as he could across the slope, climbing among stones and fir trees. The chatter of the stream faded as he left it farther behind. The rustle of the fir trees became louder and sharper. The fresh wind was swinging the treetops. The sun disappeared. A hazy cloud was stretching farther and wider across the saddened sky. The air was stuffy. The back of his coat was soaked with sweat. He had lost his striped beret somewhere and was using his hands to wipe his face, constantly scanning his surroundings and listening. At one point, he stopped to catch his breath and heard the sputtering of motorcycles, still distant but persistent. There had to be a road nearby and, sure enough, the Germans were already surrounding the area. With a sinking feeling, Ivan strained his ears, trying to figure out the best avenue of escape, and then heard some vague sound and knew that someone was running behind him.

---

*   *Russo* – Russian (Italian)

** *Häftling* – prisoner (German)

His pursuer could be a German and not a *Häftling* after all. Ivan slipped behind the mossy trunk of a fir tree, took his Browning, and clicked off the safety. The crackling of the motorcycles was getting closer. *The bastards are hemming me in,* he thought, the words flashing through his mind. Ivan looked around, dropped to one knee behind the fir tree, and lifted up his pistol. Someone's feet struck against the stones once again. He looked intensely at the place in the thicket where, he was absolutely certain, a human would appear. However, no one showed up for a while, keeping Ivan in suspense. Finally, the light, striped figure of what looked like a teenager ran out into an open space between trees. There was something lively about the figure running, looking around and glancing upwards.

"*Russo!*"

A woman? He was surprised and confused, and nearly swore in frustration. However, he was distracted by the roar of motorcycles, which had already caught up with him but were higher up the slope. Ivan spun around, uncertain where to go. He could easily be spotted here among the sparse tree trunks, and so he ducked into a small niche under a fairly steep rock and bent over, all agility and caution. The striped figure down below disappeared for a minute over the edge of the cliff, but he did not try to track it—he was more afraid of the motorcycles and was listening intently. All of a sudden, a young woman wearing an oversized coat with pulled-up sleeves and a red triangle on her chest appeared from behind a stone some twenty steps away. She quickly looked around from under a cap of longish black hair, and he noticed a joyous and lively sparkle in her equally black olive-like eyes.

*"Ciao!"**

He had already heard that word and knew that Italian *Häftlinge*** used it as a greeting. Nevertheless, he kept silent, listening to the clatter above his head and expecting her to slip somewhere for cover. Seemingly oblivious to the danger, she looked around again and began to jabber in German. As far as he could tell, she was urging someone to go away. Retracing the girl's steps with his eyes, Ivan spotted one more person in a striped uniform, who was crouching on his knees in the underbrush. In an instant, the stranger shrank back and disappeared among dense fir trees. Ivan was about to bolt to get the hell away from those *Häftlinge* when the girl popped out from behind the cliff, bent over, pushed her feet hurriedly into clogs she had been holding and click-clacked towards him.

He froze in fear. With the motorcycles roaring almost directly over their heads, her foolhardy display stabbed at his raw nerves. It was so easy to spot them! Cursing softly but sounding quite furious, Ivan stooped, leapt towards the girl, yanked her angrily by the hand, and pulled her behind the cliff. Submissive and light, she swept toward him and almost fell. There was a clatter as one of her clogs dropped on the stones and rolled away.

"Oh, *klumpes!****" she exclaimed softly.

The motorcycles were very close now, rushing past them one by one, showering them with their noisy rattle. Neither that nor his obvious anger appeared to matter to her, for she wrenched her hand free and made a beeline for her lost

---

*   *Ciao* – Hi! (Italian)

**   *Häftlinge* - prisoners

***   *Klumpes* – damn clogs (language mixture)

clog. Ivan gritted his teeth as she slipped beyond his reach. Meanwhile, she deftly grabbed the clog, darted back and gave him a quick, seemingly guilty look. Her eyes lit up with excitement and the willfulness of a spoilt and reckless little girl. And then, unable to control his jangling nerves and overwhelmed with belated anger, he slapped her on her cheek.

The girl gave a soft cry but did not recoil. She fell on a nearby rock and looked at him from under her elbow, her eyes full of some mischievous surprise, not fury.

Ivan could hear that the motorcycles were leaving and instantly regretted his outburst. She grew cautious for a moment, eyes round, ears alert, as if she had only just woken up to the danger facing them. Drawing up her knee, clad with the same striped cloth he was wearing, she pulled on her clog. And then she looked at him and repeated his curses, shaping her words like a child learning to speak and mispronouncing her consonants.

That was as unexpected as the slap on her face. So startled was Ivan that something moved and stirred inside of him—something human flooded his grief-hardened heart for a moment, and his eyes widened in surprise for the first time that day.

"Wow!"

"Wow!" she repeated the word like a tease, apparently affecting hurt, and then looked at him with some interest—indeed, with a twinkle in her eye.

The dark beauty of the girl and her singular bravery in their situation, a difficult one, to say the least, were making him confused.

"Where are you running to?" he asked sternly, looking down at her spindly drawn-up legs and clogs on her feet.

"*Was?*""

"*Was, was!* Where are you running?"

"*Russo* run, *ich*** run."

He shot a sharp, distrustful look at her, but her face was all attention and eagerness to understand him. Joined in the middle, her thick black brows were raised high over the bridge of her nose.

"You know where I'm running? I'm *Russland* running. It'll be bang, bang if I'm caught. And you'll be like this," he flicked his finger across his neck and pointed up.

She gave a quick smile, and Ivan actually thought that he had heard her snort. *I'll hang? So what?* she seemed to be saying. He almost lost his temper over her thoughtless frivolity.

"A hero, are you? A daredevil? Run then! But without me."

"Of course," the girl smiled amicably, and Ivan thought that she had misunderstood him.

He was about to tell her that when shouting and barking broke out near the town—the Germans were probably hunting for someone. "To hell with this girl," Ivan thought. It was time to move on, and he started hurriedly up the slope.

---

*   *Was?* – what? (German)

**   *Ich* - I (German)

3.

A hazy blue-grey cloud blotted out the sky. The tops of the fir trees were swaying rhythmically. The forest was noisy and agitated, and the first raindrops criss-crossed the air.

Ivan was climbing nimbly among tree trunks and stones, anxious not to slow down. He noticed now that his knee was showing through a hole in his trousers that had been made by the dog. The cloth must have stuck to a wound on the thigh while he had been standing under the rock. It came loose from walking, and the wound now hurt. His bare toes had struck so many stones that they were also bleeding now. Some thorns had ground painfully into his heel, but he had no time to think about his pain.

Meanwhile, all the noise behind his back had died down. Caught in the rain, the danger had hidden somewhere and fallen behind. He could not hear any sounds of pursuit. But they would be coming back. Ivan knew that the Germans would not just leave them alone. They had probably put all guards, policemen and dogs on alert. It would be very difficult to escape, except perhaps if the rain intervened to hide and muffle their footsteps and wash away their footprints. Ivan kept peering though the thin, misty lacework of rain with a sharp, nervous gaze, fearful of some ambush. From time to time, he also heard the footsteps of his companion. She would fall behind, lose her right or left clog or the other and then run to catch up with him. For a few minutes, he would hear her rapid, tired breathing right beside him, and then she would disappear again.

He tried to be indifferent to her. He would have probably breathed a sigh of relief if she had dropped completely out of sight, but he could not abandon or drive her away while she was nearby. He just thought how unlucky he had been to run into her. Incredibly, she had found her way out of the factory, caught up with him and was keeping pace however fast he walked. Of course, he had wasted a lot of time on the dogs and was fortunate that the Germans had been delayed and had not yet stumbled upon the gully. Meanwhile, the rain was getting heavier, and the shroud of warm fog around the wooded mountains was becoming thicker—he felt lucky, for it would now be easier for them to hide in the forest, conceal their tracks from the dogs, and get as far away from the town as possible.

Unfortunately, the rain made their walk very tiring. His soaking wet coat felt disgusting as it clung to his body. His trousers were also wet from the bottom up, and he rolled them up to the knees, the way men did in his village while mowing grass. At first he thought with satisfaction that the rain would obscure and darken his bright striped clothes and make them less visible from the distance. And so it did, but the damned circles of the glue paint targets on his chest continued to stick out of his coat. Instead of getting wet, they became even more noticeable against the blackened fabric.

After an hour or more of picking his way among wet branches linked by tightly wound cobweb strings and studded with trembling droplets, Ivan finally saw a road. Glistening with rain, the smooth stretch of the road curved slightly before disappearing into the mountains. He stopped to listen, but the road seemed empty. Then he looked back and saw the girl, who was peeling wet branches away from her face as she made her way towards him. He had to wait for her to cross the road together in case she did something wrong and exposed them both.

The girl caught up with him and stopped, tired. Having also noticed the road, she was now acting more cautiously than before. He took a cursory glance at her wet striped coat, which clung tightly to her lithe slender waist and small pointed breasts, and scowled—that was so inappropriate in their precarious situation! The girl, however, looked happy to rest. She drew her breath, steadying herself against the top of a small pine tree with one hand and emptying the water-filled clogs with the other, and gave a weary but still rather lighthearted sigh.

Feeling her fiddling at his side, he waited patiently until she was finished and then headed towards the road. Quieter now and probably tired, she started after him.

He stopped near the road again, got to his knees behind a rock, looked around, and then rose and jumped over to a concrete ditch. Fully in control of his body and keenly aware of the danger, he bent over, shouted, "Come here!" and held out his hand. Without a word, she grabbed his fingers and jumped, her clogs thudding against the concrete. "Kick them off!" he said abruptly. Guessing what he had in mind, she took off, took off the wooden shoes and grabbed them with her free hand.

Hand in hand they ran out onto the road paved with wet concrete slabs. The drizzle was quickly washing away their wet footprints. They ran over to the other side of the road, and he released her hand. She had probably stepped on prickly crushed stone as soon as she cleared the other ditch, for she gave a soft cry, threw up her hand, shoved her feet into the clogs and quickly began to climb after him.

The slope was rather steep there, interspersed with stretches of sheer rockface and covered with crooked young pine trees. No matter how high they climbed, the curving road continued to shimmer through their tops. Ivan was now paying little attention to the pace—he was very tired himself and felt that the girl, hardly tough by nature, was also running out of energy. As he lay under a sprawling spindly pine tree, recovering after a particularly steep climb and watching his climbing companion, he saw one of the clogs fall off her feet and roll downhill among the stones. "*Porca Madonna!*" she cursed, looked back, and sat down, apparently hesitant to go after it because of fatigue. A moment later, however, she was limping down on one foot and picking up the clog. When she looked up at Ivan, he saw relief and quiet gratitude in her eyes for not leaving her alone. He sat down on the dry, prickly ground among twisted roots and waited until she cleared the slope and dropped beside him in exhaustion.

"Why don't you throw the damn things away?" he said, thinking about the clogs.

He pointed at them and let his hands drop when she looked questioningly at him. She shook her head and simultaneously shifted her small, wet foot. It looked very delicate, and he immediately saw both how inappropriate his advice had been and how much trouble her oversized wooden shoes would be.

Why, even the soles of his own feet, cut by prickly stones and branches, were literally on fire. His left foot was particularly bad. Subconsciously drawing out his minute of rest, he looked at his rain-washed sole to check what was wrong with it.

"*Russo* very, very *furioso?* How is it *Deutsch*? *Böse*," the girl suddenly asked.

After a year of captivity, Ivan could understand basic German and knew what she had said but did not answer at once. He tried to pull out a splinter from his heel, but its tiny tip just would not stay between his fingers.

"*Böse!* You will be *böse* when push comes to shove," he said unkindly and finally answered, "Why *böse?* I *gut****."

"*Gut?*"

She smiled, smoothed her wet radiant hair with both hands, rubbed her palms on her trousers and moved towards him on her knees.

"Oh, let me!"

Try as he might, he could not get hold of the end of the splinter. And so she bent over with eagerness and surprising simplicity, like a friend, clasped his huge foot with her cold thin hands, picked at it with her fingers, and, before he knew it, bit his sole with her teeth. He pulled his foot away hesitantly, but it remained in her hands as her teeth scraped over the thick skin on his heel. When she straightened out, a black splinter was pinched between her white even teeth.

Ivan was not surprised, nor did he thank her. He drew up his foot, looked at the heel and tried to put his weight on it—the pain seemed to have eased. Now he regarded the girl and her wet, swarthy, now livelier face with more favour than before. Meeting his gaze and never averting her

---

*　　　*Deutsch* – German (German)

**　　　*furioso (Italian), böse (German)* - angry

***　　　*Gut* – good (German)

twinkly eyes, she picked the splinter with her fingers and flicked it into the wind.

"Resourceful, all right," he said reservedly, as if reluctant to admit the girl's virtues.

"Re-sus-fol," she repeated merrily and asked, "What is resusfol?"

He smiled to himself and scratched his shaven wet head with his hand.

"Well, how do they say it? *Gut,* in short."

"*Gut?*"

"*Ja*.* Gut.*"

"*Du** gut, ich gut,*" she said joyfully and laughed.

As if recalling or weighing something in his mind, he took a longer look at her than before, but she immediately lost her short-lived gaiety, shivered, and he thought that it was time to go. Although very reluctant to leave their dry shelter under the sprawling pine tree and get wet again, he forced himself to get up. Droplets of rain were falling in unison all around them, the forest was rustling monotonously. Foul weather must have disrupted the Germans' search party, much to the fugitives' relief. No one knew how many prisoners had made it into the mountains. Hopefully, at least some of them would be lucky. Remembering that third *Häftling* who had almost joined them, Ivan turned towards the girl as she was emptying her clogs and then took a step away from the pine tree.

"And who was the lad running behind you?"

"Running, yes? *Häftling. Tedesco**** Häftling.*"

---

*　　　　*ja* – yes (German)

**　　　*du* – you (German)

***　　*tedesco* – German (Italian)

"An acquaintance? A friend?"

"*Non* friend. *Krank*[*] *Häftling*. Ill." She touched her temple with her skinny finger.

"Mad?"

"*Ja*."

We can understand each other, can't we? he thought with satisfaction and looked away. For some reason, he was still uncomfortable looking into her deep, wide open eyes, whose expression changed so often to reflect and exude her varied emotions.

"All right. To hell with him. Let's go."

It looked like they had got quite far away from the camp, and the Germans had lost track of them. The tension within him eased a little, and Ivan thought back with some odd detachment and surprise to what had happened during that crazy day.

---

[*] *krank* – sick (German)

4.

In the morning the five of them were digging up an unexploded bomb in a workshop that had been half destroyed by a night bombing raid.

They were *Häftlinge,* or *Flugpünkte*[*], to be more precise. There in the death camp they had lost almost all hope of survival, and the only thing they still wanted was to make a break for freedom for one last time, or, to quote their loudmouth, a small dark lad nicknamed Zhuk, to slam the door on the way out of this world.

Not very safe and definitely not easy, their work was nevertheless nearing completion.

Prying under the bomb with crowbars, they finally extracted it from under the crushed stone and, holding it by the stabilizing fin, carefully placed it on lumps of earth inside the hole. Now came the most risky and important part. While the others stood around with bated breath, a handy fellow nicknamed Golodai, a former Black Sea sailor who wore a standard striped coat with bright circles on the chest and back, put a handpicked spanner over the fuse. The cords in his bared muscular forearms swelled with exertion, the veins on his temples stood out, and the fuse moved a little. Golodai turned the spanner two more times and then

---

[*] *Flugpünkte* – live targets that could be shot for the slightest misdemeanour (German)

knelt and began to unscrew the fuse hurriedly with his hands. It had been severely damaged by the impact and could no longer perform its deadly function in the bomb, which had been dropped the previous night from an American B-29 or a British Mosquito. Those planes had nearly flattened this mountain-squeezed Austrian town. However, despite its faulty fuse, the bomb itself had not been disabled and continued to hold an explosive power equivalent of 500 kilogrammes of TNT. That power was the hope of the five condemned men. As soon as the bomb had been defused, Zhuk leaned over Golodai, slid his hand under his coat, pulled out a new-looking fuse which had been salvaged the day before from a broken finless bomb, and started to screw it into the empty socket with his thin, nervous fingers.

However, the lad was being hasty, missing the threads and causing the metal to clang. Ivan rose slightly in his clogs and looked over the fresh earth in case someone stumbled upon them. Fortunately, everything seemed to be quiet. Twisted girders were dangling from the ceiling, beams of light were filtering through the numerous cracks overhead and falling on the floor at sharp angles. The room was steamy, sunny and dusty. He could hear occasional cries and muted conversation from behind a row of concrete supports, where dozens of people who were stirring and milling about in the sunlit dust as they pulled the rubble apart. They were watched over by SS officers, who cared little for bomb disposal and normally stayed away from such operations.

"All right, bastards, just you wait!" Zhuk said in a quiet voice, barely controlling a fury that was bubbling just under the surface.

"Keep your mouth shut, don't rush things," Golodai growled as he got back to his feet.

"It's alright, brothers, it's alright," Yanushka said in the corner, wiping his wet forehead. A former *kolkhoz** manager, he was now a one-eyed *Häftling* decorated with chest targets for three attempts to escape.

He was an optimist by nature, if, indeed, a POW can be optimistic, and always reassured everybody, despite his missing eye and his burst spleen. He was reassuring both when he was telling people to escape and when he was being brought back to the camp under convoy, debilitated by torture and his clothes shredded by Alsatian dogs.

Each man had by now shown what he thought of the plan, except, perhaps, for Srebnikau, who was standing aloof, near an earth wall, and coughing as he always did, and Ivan. From the very beginning, Srebnikau had not been thrilled about their scheme. The man would obviously have little to celebrate even if they succeeded—consumption was killing him faster than the camp and the deprivations he suffered in it. As for Ivan Tsyareshka, he simply cared nothing for small talk and did not like to prattle when everything was clear anyway.

Meanwhile Golodai wiped his palms on his striped trousers and looked at the other men— he was the obvious leader there.

" Who's going to hit the fuse?"

For a few seconds they all fell silent, lowered their eyes and peered in embarrassment at the long cigar-shaped 500-kilogramme bomb and sweeping scratches on its

---

*   *kolkhoz* – collective farm (Russian)

green sides. That was probably their biggest problem, and it made everyone uncomfortable. Yanushka's sad face with grey stubble and sunken cheeks grew focused. The nervous determination in Zhuk's flinty eyes faded. As for Srebnikau, he even stopped coughing and stretched his arms down his wafer-thin body. His gaze was now unbearably mournful. The question they had pondered, feared and avoided from the very beginning, struggling to make up their minds, was clearly forcing them to suppress painful and uneasy sadness in their hearts.

Whatever they felt, Golodai's broad face expressed severity and steely determination.

"There're no volunteers," he concluded grimly. "Let's draw then."

"Yes, that's right," Zhuk said, eyes brightening, and took a step toward ringleader Golodai.

"Okay, let's draw," Yanushka agreed.

Srebnikau coughed stiffly but sounded relieved. Without a word, Tsyareshka drove the end of a crowbar into the ground in one thrust. All of a sudden, Golodai slapped himself on the thigh. "What are we going to draw? We don't have any matches or straws."

He looked around thoughtfully and grabbed a heavy sledgehammer with a long handle.

"Now then. Grip it higher."

He crouched and gripped the handle right next to the head. The other men moved closer to him and leaned over the sledgehammer, pressing their heads against each other. Zhuk was the first to grasp the handle. Yanushka's gnarled fingers closed over it next, followed by Srebnikau's palm, then Tsyareshka's paw, then Golodai's, Zhuk's and Yanushka's hands. When only a thin strip of wood was visible under the tangle of fingers, Srebnikau's shaky, clammy hand slowly touched the tip of the shaft.

The others breathed a sigh of relief, rose to their feet and stood near the walls for half a minute, trying not to look at each other.

Golodai passed the sledgehammer to the one who was destined to die with it.

"Everything was fair, no cheating," Golodai said, still rather crudely but with a touch of sympathy.

For some reason, Srebnikau stopped coughing, staggered, took the handle, turned it around silently, tried to pick up the sledgehammer, and then let it go. He looked miserably at the lads.

"I can't detonate the bomb," he said in a quiet voice of a condemned man. "I wouldn't manage."

Everyone fell silent again. Golodai flashed an angry look at the poor wreck.

"What are you talking about?"

"I can't detonate it. I'm getting too weak," Srebnikau explained sadly and let loose with a violent, painful cough.

"Well, well," Zhuk said in frustration. "We're back to square one."

"That's the way it goes. Of course, how could he detonate it? He's too weak." Yanushka was ready to accept what had happened.

Something in Tsyareshka's heart turned upside down. Although he understood that Srebnikau was telling the truth, this unexpected turn of event had enraged him. For about a minute, he glowered at the wretch, making some decision. Naturally, he did not want to die. He had always longed to live, tried to break free three times and almost reached Zhytomyr on one occasion. And yet, there are clearly moments in life when all the resilience built over the years is not enough for one decisive moment. Without more ado Ivan took a step towards Srebnikau.

"Give it to me."

Srebnikau's mournful eyelids fluttered in surprise, and his fingers readily released the handle. Tsyareshka moved the sledgehammer and suddenly took charge, speaking in a cautious voice, slightly embarrassed by their dithering.

"What are you standing there for? Let's pick it up. What are we waiting for?"

The stern Golodai, the nervous Zhuk, the anxious Yanushka glanced at him in puzzlement and then, hope rising in their hearts, stepped up to the bomb.

"Grab it! Zhuk, get the rope! Bring the joists! Where have you put them?" Tsyareshka was shouting orders with unnatural fluency and looked out of the pit in search of the sticks they had saved for the occasion.

His companions probably saw his eyes flinch and stopped dead in their tracks, while Tsyareshka, sensing disaster, straightened up and froze.

Standing some distance away from the pit in a dusty stream of slanting sun rays was *Kommandoführer* Sandler. He looked across the workshop intently and nodded when their eyes met.

"*Komm!*"

Tsyareshka swore to himself, propped the sledgehammer against a wall, and quickly climbed its steep surface to the loose soil at the top, knowing that it would be dangerous to delay. The lads behind him fell silent and held their breath.

------

*   *komm!* – come! (German)

That part of the dusty workshop was empty—afraid of the unexploded bomb, the Germans had immediately pulled out the machine tools. The facility was stuffy, awash in the dusty rays of midday sunshine that flooded the interior through the broken ceiling. The other ruined section of that enormous hangar-like structure was swarming with dozens of women deployed from Sector C to clear the rubble. They carried debris and stretchers and pushed wheelbarrows laden with crushed stone along a planked path on the floor.

Sandler was standing in the path, away from a huge patch of light on the concrete floor, and waiting with his hands behind his back. Tsyareshka's clogs made a loud clattering sound as he scurried down the earth pile. The noise died down when he stopped five steps away from Sandler right in the middle of the light patch, creasing his wide brows. The SS officer withdrew one hand from behind his back and pulled the peak of his cap with his fingers.

"*Wie ist mit der Bombe?**"

"Soon. *Bald. Gleich***," Ivan replied in a hunted voice.

"*Schneller hinauslegen*****!*"

Sandler glanced suspiciously in the direction of the pit and at the tense faces of the men staring out of it. Then he took a probing look at Ivan, who was standing rigidly upright, like a soldier ready for anything. There was little he could take for granted with targets on his coat. His eyes peered intently at the clean-shaven, pleasantly tanned face of the German, who was probably not much older than him,

---

*   *Wie ist mit der Bombe?*- How's it going with the bomb? (German)

**   *Bald. Gleich* – Soon. Right away (German)

***   *Schneller hinauslegen* – Get it out quick (German) full of the sense of power and Aryan dignity. He cautiously watched every movement of Sandler's fearsome hands out of the corner of his eye. In the distance, at the other end of the workshop, two women in striped clothes put their stretcher down on the floor and waited with fear and apparent interest to see what would happen next. Luckily, the German gave the stiff and poised Ivan only a fleeting glance and dropped his guard, apparently interpreting Ivan's outward readiness for action according to his own lights. Having nothing else to say to this *Flugpunkt,* he put one foot forward.

"I vont zem shinink," he said in an odd mixture of Russian and German and nodded at a fresh layer of dust on his boot.

Although he had heard that order before and definitely understood what was expected of him, Ivan was slightly disoriented by its suddenness and hesitated for a second. However, with Sandler waiting with a menacingly cold expression on his square-jawed face, a long delay was out of the question, and Ivan crouched beside his feet. That was humiliating, offensive, and it took all his will power to stifle the stubborn rage that was building in his heart and could be so unhelpful now.

Ivan stooped low and began to shine the boots with the stretched sleeves of his striped coat. The boots were new, made of box calf leather and seemed to have been carefully waxed in the morning. The bright sunshine was soon glinting off the toecap of the first boot. Before long, the whole boot was shining. Only the welt still had some leftover dust, and a fresh scratch would not disappear from the tip of the toe. Meanwhile, the *Kommandoführer* flicked his cigarette lighter, lit up and put the cigarette case in his pocket. A puff of smoke stung his nostrils, and the German shook ashes from his cigarette, sending sparks over Ivan's shaven head. A burning particle singed his neck, and a wave of fury surged through Ivan's jangled nerves. He barely resisted an urge to jump to his feet, hit that bastard, knock him to the floor and trample him underfoot. By an effort of will, he forced himself to his task, anxious to get rid of the German as soon as possible. Sandler, however, was in no hurry and did not withdraw his boot until it was shining from the toecap to the knee. When Ivan was finished, he put forward the other foot.

Ivan straightened his back. In the brief moment of respite, he took his first look at the female *Häftlinge*, who were watching him over the boots. He ran his eyes over them very quickly, almost absent-mindedly. All of a sudden, something caused him to start. Ivan looked at the women more closely, trying to understand his own reaction, and then he saw it all. Immediately, he felt that he would rather go up in smoke than face the withering contempt in that pair of enormous eyes. For some reason, he did not even notice anything else or see whether the face was young or old—the unbearable reproach in that glance splashed agony into his heart. Meanwhile, the other dusty boot with a lime stain on the top slid towards his knees. As he lingered, the German muttered impatiently and poked Ivan in the chest with his toecap. Whatever still allowed Ivan to hold his temper now failed, causing his fingers to let go of his sleeves and his fingernails to dig themselves into his palms.

In one swift motion, he jumped to his feet. Propelled by a vicious force that made his fists unbearably heavy, he landed a wild blow on the German's jaw. Everything happened so quickly and unexpectedly that he was actually surprised to see Sandler's white Adam's apple swing upwards and his peaked cap fly off his head as the SS officer landed on the concrete floor with a thud.

Still unable to fully grasp the awful consequences of that incident, Ivan stood in front of the German with his fists clenched, his head lowered and his feet wide apart. He expected the German to bounce right back to his feet and pounce on him. He heard excited shouts in the distance but was too disoriented to tell whether they were meant to shame or warn him. Contrary to his expectations, the SS officer did not pounce. He appeared to be struggling with pain as he gingerly rolled over on his side, sat up, collected his cap and dusted it off. It looked like he was in no hurry to get up. Sitting with his legs wide apart, one of his boots shiny and the other one dirty, he smoothed his hair with his hand and carefully put his peaked cap back on. Then he raised his eyes to give the stunned and obviously confused *Flugpunkt* a dark, sinister look and resolutely pulled the leather strip on the holster at his side.

For a split second, Ivan thought that everything was lost, but he had no time to feel frustration—the bolt of the pistol clacked nearby and the German sprang to his feet with surprising agility. However dazed Ivan had been for half a minute, he now snapped right out of his stupor, lowered his head and charged at his enemy, not wanting to die in vain.

He never got to the German. A massive explosion erupted nearby, throwing Ivan into the air and deafening him. The Earth rocked, heaved and plunged him into the blackness of an abyss. A cloud of red dust covered the German and everything around him.

In a second, Ivan felt that he was lying on the floor. Something was still crumbling and falling on either side of him, something was sizzling in noxious smoke, burning his back. A brick fell and shattered next to him in oddly slow motion.

Feeling that he was alive, Ivan spun deftly on the floor and looked around. The familiar boot with a scratch on its toe was scrabbling on the concrete beside him. The enemy's form was wriggling in the streams of dust, trying to crawl away. Ivan snatched a handy chunk of concrete, swung his heavy weapon and thrust it into the German's back. Sandler twitched, moaned and flailed his arm in the air, and Ivan remembered about the pistol. He swept over the German on his knees, tore the Browning from his weakened fingers and rushed into the whirling cloud of red dust that had already shrouded the workshop, his heart pounding furiously in his chest.

5.

The gloomy, inhospitable night overtook the fugitives in a rocky ravine, which was overgrown with crooked pine trees and gradually tapered as it climbed the gentle slope.

Not so brisk now, Ivan was climbing mossy stones, stopping from time to time to wait for the girl, who was stubbornly plodding on despite her exhaustion. He thought that it would be better for them to get out of that bleak ravine. The terrain had to be smoother and the darkness that was filling the hollow like a murky fog had to be thinner on higher ground. Unfortunately, Ivan was also running out of energy and no longer had the will for such a move. And then, he was very anxious to put as much distance as he could between himself and the town and make the best of that fortuitously rainy evening, which had hidden their two sets of footprints from Alsatians so well. Gradually, he climbed farther and higher into the mountains. Only there, in the Alps, there could be at least some safety. On the roads and in the valleys down below there was death.

Those damned mountains! He was grateful to them for being inaccessible to German guards with dogs, motorcycles and checkpoints, but he was also beginning to hate them for their ability to drain energy so relentlessly and wear a traveler out so completely. That was so unlike his previous time on the run, his escape from Silesia. How convenient its plains, fields and meadows were for walking at night, as stars in the sky showed him the way home! Sneaking into German villages and farmsteads to find some food, they stole vegetables and milk jugs lined up near farm gates, ready to be sent to the town in the morning. All day long they would hide in crop fields or among trees, guarding each other in turns as the surprisingly testing hours of inaction dragged on. Danger still lurked everywhere. For a whole month, their small group of ragged, unshaven, ghastly-looking men made their way towards their native country. Whatever happened to his mates, he had very bad luck. After his escape, he fell into the hands of real monsters, who were even worse than the Germans while looking like his kith and kin.

While they were driving him to the town, he could hardly believe that they were not joking, those common country lads who wore plain peasant shirts and jackets, carried only shotguns and looked so good-hearted as they swore lazily in an intelligible language. Only the one with a white arm band had a carbine slung over his shoulder. Their chief, Hryts, was also armed with a carbine.

And now, the mountains, the Lechtal Alps, an unknown, mysterious, unseen land that offered a slim hope of freedom and reunion with his own people.

Just when he grew too tired and started looking for a place to rest, Ivan heard a thud behind his back and saw stones roll down the cliff. He glanced over his shoulder. Leaning on her hands, the girl was lying on the slope, making no apparent effort to get up. He also stopped, straightened up, drew his breath, and waited. The ravine was getting dark. Barely perceptible droplets of rain were falling from the sky like fine dust. The grey contours of stones were almost indistinguishable from their surroundings. The disheveled strands of fir trees stood black against the sky. Clouds hung low over the ground, overloaded with darkness and rainwater. His wet clothes were warm from walking and a little clammy, and shivers were running up and down his moist back, signalling that it was time to stop. In the distance, he saw the dark limp form of his companion, the weak movements of her head and her motionless arms, bare to the elbows. She did not get up. At last, he forced himself to go down, slid the Browning under his coat, bent over and carefully lifted her light, thin body under her armpits. She stirred under his touch and sat up without raising her head. He stood still and thought with sadness that that would probably have to be the end of the first day of their journey, and they would have to spend their night in that gully.

He looked around. A jumble of cliffs and stones rose steeply on one side. On the other, the slope fell away to blend with the dark clutter of pine trees. Gloomy damp fog was creeping from the valley in an endless stream. Ivan could no longer tell its depth—he was only able to hear the distant gurgle of the brook coming from its grey, stuffy silence.

With a tap on her shoulder, Ivan motioned her to wait and then walked forward, still trying to get his bearings in the gloom. There was a slight overhang in the rocky slope that could afford some protection. Sure enough, the shelter was not very impressive or secure, but a road-weary traveller is grateful for any cover over his head.

He gingerly walked back to the girl over sharp stones.

She had just been so vivacious, so playfully reckless in front of the motorcyclists. Where was all that now? She looked like a tired wet bird that had ended up among those stones by some weird quirk of fate. Breathing heavily, she did not react to his touch or get up. Instead, she curled even more tightly into a small, stubborn ball and trembled.

"Let's go and get some rest," he said. "Rest, you understand? Sleep a little, huh?"

For a moment, the girl grew still and stopped shivering, but she did not get up and continued to sit with her head hung low. He waited a little longer and then scooped her up under her knees, intending to carry her to the shelter. Suddenly, she pulled against his grip with surprising force, exclaimed in Italian, kicked, and broke free. *To hell with you! Sit here, if you're so touchy,* he thought angrily after a few awkward seconds. Climbing under the rock, he tossed aside the sharper stones, sat down and immediately lost all his strength. For the first time, Ivan felt how weak he was. Without opening his eyes, he pulled the collar of his coat higher over the back of his head and fell asleep.

The world immediately ceased to exist for him, giving way to a chaotic flurry of nightmares. As always, that shift was so subtle that it appeared to be a natural extension of the horror of the daytime. He had had the same dream for more than a year, experiencing pain that was nothing short of real almost every night, the subconscious, subjectively transformed horrors of one day of war, which had impacted him with such brutal force and had probably left an indelible imprint on his tortured mind.

Everything started with a very real, very painful sense of impending doom, which could only be a foretaste of utter defeat. Although that immense disaster had been driven and blotted out of his conscious mind by other disasters, great and small, it continued to torment him in his dreams with unrelenting force, apparently multiplied by countless subsequent misfortunes.

As always, a wall of a shabby Ukrainian clay house loomed large in the first act of this dream. Written in coal on its corner were the words "Oleksiyiv's Prop." with an arrow under them pointing the way to that property. Needless to say, the writing was a month old, made while the army had still been advancing on Zmiiv, bypassing Kharkiv. Now, however, all the troops were moving in the opposite direction. At night, they had ditched road tractors in the river for lack of gasoline, scattered disassembled gun locks around the field, burnt staff records in the garden. At dawn, after a brief officer meeting, the colonel who commanded the surrounded group had shot himself dead in the yard that was now their shelter. Their company had been ordered to cover the retreating troops, and three soldiers led by a crestfallen lieutenant had dug out a narrow trench near that hut, which was situated on the edge of the village.

That was seared into his memory forever. However, in the torturous fumes of his sleep, the colonel was alive. He was darting about the yard with a map-board in his hands and cursing Golodai, who had turned from a Black Sea sailor into the commander of an assault rifle company. It is also unclear why *Flugpunkt* Srebnikau and not Abdurakhmanov, a private in their vanquished battery who knew almost no Russian, is sitting in the trench together with sergeant Tsyareshka.

Instead of getting his machine gun ready for battle, the wretch is feverishly scraping his *Flugpunkt* targets off his shirt with a German hatchet and mumbling, "Not a step back! Not a step back!" And yet, there is nothing unreal about his next memory of that distant morning—the clear spring sky is giving birth to a sunny day, the clay house casts a cool blueish shadow across the road, nettles and weeds under the fence are quivering, shedding dew on the ground, and an upturned pot drying out on a fence picket is jiggling and vibrating. And the road near the village is crawling with tanks. They should appear from behind this house any moment, but Ivan Tsyareshka just cannot insert the fuse into a grenade. He pushes it with his fingers as hard as he can, but the small yellow cylinder will not enter the hole, as if it was deliberately made too thick. Tsyareshka gets nervous and hasty and strikes it with his fist, risking an explosion. When he comes to his senses, he sees that he is alone in the trench, that all his friends have abandoned him. And then something happens, and he realises that he ought to escape, that he has not heard any order to retreat. Ivan throws his chest against the parapet, knocking some dirt loose, tries to get out of the trench, but his legs feel strangely heavy and unresponsive, causing him to slide back.

And the tanks are now around the corner.

Startled by their rumbling, a huge flock of sparrows dart into the air from the shelter of vegetable gardens, filling half the sky, and veer sharply to the left and then to the right in their coordinated flight. Finally, a tank rolls into view from around the corner, tearing the ground as it turns, and Ivan realises that he will not manage to escape.

In a stupor he swings the grenade and throws it onto the road. However, instead of exploding, the grenade bounces and hisses between the two ruts as the tank is about to pass it. Fear grips Ivan. Meanwhile, the tank crew spots the trench near the wall. The tank swerves on one track, and then unspeakable terror fills his heart—the tank turns out to be a Soviet T-34.

The realisation of what he has done paralyzes Ivan for a second. Then he spins around, leaps back and nearly impales his face on a broad, gleaming knife bayonet. The

German takes a quick step toward Ivan, and the bayonet smoothly cuts through his chest, as if it belongs to someone else's body. Ivan knows that this is the end, that he is dead and almost chokes with despair, despite feeling absolutely no pain for some reason.

At that point, he usually wakes up from sheer terror. This time, however, his mind continues to exist in some disembodied state and reassures him that this is not the end yet, that captivity and escape still lie ahead. That is why he cannot die, even though he has been pierced with a bayonet.

Ivan does not even notice the change when these sleep ghosts leave and others appear. Now he finds himself in a village, in his Tsyareshki, in the ancient land of the Kryvich tribe*. The war has apparently not begun yet, and he has not even been conscripted into the army. Along a muddy street, riddled with the hoof prints of sheep, he is running towards a kolkhoz barn on the outskirts. He knows that Golodai and several other *Häftlinge* were goaded into the barn with their hands tied. Ivan's heart is bursting with resentment and exertion. It looks like he will be late and never prove to others that they should not take their anger out on prisoners, that their captivity is not their fault but their misfortune, that they did not surrender but were captured.

Unfortunately, he never reaches the barn. His bare feet sink into the heavy, sticky mud, he can barely move them, as well as his hands and the whole body. His progress is so slow and difficult that running feels like wading through water. Looking for a better way to go, he turns towards the fence and suddenly sees someone's long shins and bare feet. He throws his head back—sitting on the top rail is an unfamiliar

---

*   The earliest inhabitants of what is now Belarus

girl with black, arched eyebrows and a snow-white dress. She gives him a joyful, radiant smile with her black eyes, which resemble ripe plums, and says, "*Ciao*, Ivan!"

He stops, suddenly forgetting his mates and everything else on God's green Earth. He is delighted and embarrassed to meet with her, a perfect stranger who feels like an old acquaintance, for she is the one who has inhabited his unconscious dreams all his youth. Overwhelmed with joy, he throws himself towards the fence, towards her. And immediately, he looks at himself and bites his lip—he has just returned from his work, from the field, from the tractor, he is wearing old trousers with patched knees and a shirt frayed on the shoulders. Embarrassed, he stops and frowns. The happy smile also disappears from her uncommonly sunny face, the whiteness of her dress fades, and she gradually vanishes, like a ghost.

Ivan lunges towards the fence, grabs the rails and rips out vine-wrapped posts. Suddenly, Ivan's mother appears in front of him. Resting her hands on that top rail, she stands quietly in the potato field on the other side, clad all in peasant dark, and tells him mournfully, "A Nazi, that's who she is. She's reported your boys to the police."

"Where is she? Where is she?" he wants to shout but cannot because there is a rope around his neck—a black silk cord that was always used in the camp to hang prisoners to the beat of drums. The rope is tightening and stretching, and its other end is dragging like the leash behind the Alsatian, the one he did not finish off in the creek. Alive and strong, the Alsatian pulls hard, and he falls, tries to shout, but his voice fails. And then he wakes up from some inner jolt.

6.

"Ha-ha-ha!" A ringing, carefree laugh echoes over them.

Ivan raises his head, feels his neck, opens his sleepy eyes wide, and catches his first glimpse of a new morning—the bright, deep blues of a clear sky juxtaposed by the striking white-toothed radiance of the girl's smile.

"*Basta schlafen**. March-march now," she says.

A cold-induced cramp shot through Ivan's body like a bolt of electricity. He kept silent for a while, struggling to return to the real, turbulent world, and met her restrained gaiety with a suspicious gaze. Giulia was sitting near him and biting on a blade of grass that must have been used to tickle him awake.

"Did you say march? Well, we'll see."

"*Sì, sì***," she agreed, studying his face with a sly spark in her eye.

He shivered again, jumped to his feet and began waving his arms furiously, swinging his legs from side to side and squatting, the way soldiers do to get warm. Giulia looked surprised at first, her arched brows raised high over her eyes, and then she suddenly burst out laughing, so loudly that he panicked even though the noise did not last long.

____

*   *Basta schlafen* – enough sleep (Italian and German)

**   *sì* – yes (Italian)

"Quiet!"

She fell silent, looked around and pressed her palm against her mouth, but unruly, mischievous imps were already jumping in her eyes. He glanced at her with sternness and disapproval and listened, feeling warmth and fatigue fill his numb body. She gave another soft, benign chuckle.

"*Ist das Gymnastik?*"*

"Yes, it is. Why, is it better to be cold?"

Ivan looked worried and generally reluctant to talk. Giulia must have noticed his mood, for she grew more serious, let her narrow skinny shoulders twitch from cold under her moist coat, let out a brief sigh and glanced at him with concern.

Peering around—an old army habit of his—Ivan realised that he had indeed slept for too long. The day had broken a long time ago. Although the sun had not yet risen from behind the mountains, the cloudless sky seemed to be ringing with bright blue morning colours. The grey mountain faces, the pine trees, the broad and steep scree slopes and the soaring summits on the other, bright side of the ravine were shining in all their colourful splendour. Still in the domain of night, their side of the rocks was dark and sleepy.

"*Montagne*** is good!" she said when she saw him surveying the surroundings. "How *ist das*? *Estetico****!*"

With a thump of her clogs, she leapt off her stony perch and also left their shelter, admiring the riot of sunlight

---

*   *Ist das Gymnastik?* – is that gymnastics? (German)

**   *Montagne* – mountains (Italian)

***   *Estetico* – beautiful (Italian)

on the other side of the broad ravine. Ivan, however, did not share her naive delight. As was the case almost every morning in the camp, a painful sensation of emptiness—the usual, thoroughly familiar pangs of hunger—filled his belly, chest, every smallest part of his body. Unfortunately, there was nothing to eat. He had no idea where to find food in those damned mountains and simultaneously certain that they would not last long without it. He said nothing for a bit, swallowed, and then asked, paying no attention to what she was doing, "Where will you go?"

Her eyebrows moved questioningly.

"March, march where?" he repeated, apparently beginning to lose his temper, and waved in different directions. "Here or there? Where were you going?"

"Oh, *Ostfront**, *Russo* front go."

He gave her a surprised look.

"*Sì, sì,*" she confirmed, seeing his surprise and mistrust. "*Signorina gut Krauts* bang, bang."

Frowning, Ivan peered at her face, radiant, mercurial, animated and too pretty for his taste. Was she joking? No, that did not seem to be the case. She had stated her intention and was now looking at Ivan with her huge, bottomless eyes, awaiting his response.

"You're babbling nonsense," he said, wrapping the flaps of his coat tighter around himself.

"*Was? Was ist* babble? *Russo* teach *signorina* Russian sprechen****?"

"We'll see."

---

*   *Ostfront* - Eastern front (German)

**   *Sprechen* – speak (German)

"See *ist gut. Accordo*, sì?" she pressed jokingly.

Ivan never gave a reply. He shivered again, feeling the cool wetness of the coat on his back, and glanced at the ridiculous circles of his chest targets. Indeed, they had to think about clothes as well, for they would not get very far in their striped uniforms. He hooked his fingers under the seam and ripped the triangle and the number off his coat with a snap. Following his example, she immediately started tearing off hers. But the nails on her thin fingers were too delicate, and the threads of the German badges were too strong to tear easily. And so she took a step towards him and cocked her shoulder, sticking out her puffy lower lip like a child.

"Give."

"Take, not give," he said and slowly turned towards her.

The sharp, pointed bumps under her moist coat made him frown and purse his lips. Immediately noticing his reaction, she made a fold and pulled it away from her chest. After a brief hesitation, he pinched an edge of the triangle and pulled hard. Careful not to leave behind any trace, he crumpled everything and shoved the bundle into a crack under a stone.

"*Grazie***, tank you.*"

"Where did you learn Russian?" he asked.

"*Italia. Roma* learn. Camp *Russian signorina* Marusya learn. *Gut* Russian *sprechen* I?"

"*Gut,*" he agreed reluctantly.

"Understand very better *gut,*" she boasted, and the ever-present twinkle in her eyes made him think that she was joking.

---

*   *Accordo* – agreed (Italian)

**   *Grazie* – thanks (Italian)

Ivan, however, was thinking about something else.

"We'll go to Trieste. You know where Trieste is?"

"O, Trieste! *Italia,*" she responded excitedly.

"I know it's in Italy. But where is it? This way or that?"

She looked in one direction, then the other, and waved confidently towards the mountains that screened the rising sun from view.

"*Das ist* road Trieste."

"Road!" he thought grimly. A road indeed, running across the Alps, across ravines and rivers and, most importantly, across densely populated valleys and busy highways. That partisan Trieste, a city he had heard much about in the camp, was definitely not within easy reach. However, he had little choice now, and if he had been lucky enough to break free from hell, it would now be stupid to have himself hanged by a black string to the beat of drums.

That was why he had to walk, climb, run! Pull himself together, summon all his energy, all his wits, all his abilities, cross the main ridge, find partisans—Yugoslav or Italian—do whatever it took to rejoin their ranks and take up arms. This was his dream now, his ultimate justice, and his reward for all the sufferings and shame he had experienced during the year of captivity.

The damp, gloomy ravine was chilly. After the numbing cold of the night, his body was also wracked with shivers and longing for warmth and sunshine.

Finding a more or less suitable place on the slope, they started climbing uphill among stones. For the first time since their meeting, she was in the lead while he was climbing slightly behind her, and that looked like an understanding between them and the beginnings of mutual trust.

With the slope getting quite steep now, the clogs kept slipping and falling off her feet. Halfway up, the girl took them off, gripped them in one hand and started leaping from stone to stone, nimble as a lizard, grabbing thorny tufts of some wire-hard grass with the other hand.

"*Russo*," she said without stopping. "You *ist Offizier?*"

"An officer? Come on, I'm a prisoner of war."

"Prisoner, prisoner. I understand. Who you was before war?

Ivan was slow to reply. Unhappy with her prying, he answered sullenly, "Kolkhoz worker."

"What is kolkoz worker?"

"You ask even though you don't understand," he rebuked her unkindly. "It's something like a *Bauer**. *Verstehen?***"

"Ah, understand: *Landwirtschaft?****"

"That's right. Kolkhoz."

"Oh, I love kolkoz very much!" she suddenly said with excitement. "Kolkoz is *gut. Lavorare compagnia*****. Rest *compagnia. Tutto****** *compagnia. Russo* kolkoz *gut economico, si?*" she asked and looked back.

He never gave a reply. Dislodged by her feet, stones, earth and other debris rolled downhill, barely missing him as he leaned away. She laughed over his head and pressed her side against the slope.

"Keep quiet!" Ivan hissed angrily.

---

*　　　　*Bauer* – farmer (German)

**　　　*Verstehen?* – understand? (German)

***　　*Landwirtschaft?* – agriculture? (German)

****　*Lavorare compagnia* – work together (Italian)

*****　*Tutto* – everything (Italian)

She bit her tongue again, covered her mouth with her hand and looked back.

"Pardon."

"Pardon, pardon! Be quiet. Why are you laughing your head off?"

Her recklessness was making Ivan angry. He must have been too rude to her, for she knitted her brows and pursed her lips.

"My name *ist* Giulia. Signorina Giulia," she declared.

He sized her up sternly and said to himself, *So what? Signorina!* That was of little consequence to him—he had no intention of treating her with kid gloves. She fell silent and scampered uphill, apparently nursing a grudge. Ivan, however, was in no great hurry.

Hunched low to the ground, he was taking long strides, planting his sore toes on cold rough stones, glancing from under his brow at her agile striped figure and wondering who she was. Some European *Hure**, as the Germans say, a homeless drifter from chaotic Italian cities, a thoughtless butterfly whose life had been ravaged by war? That seemed to be the best answer considering her exuberance and apparent hunger for adventure. Yes, her triangle was red, political, and she had said something about hatred for the Nazis. Some German might have hurt her, and then she had obviously had a rough time in the camp. However, do people like her carry grudges? Of course, he knew almost nothing about her, but she had repeatedly proven to be light-hearted and thoughtless about many things that would make or break their attempt to escape. Ivan understood full well that he had to be extra vigilant under such circumstances and mostly rely on himself.

---

*   *Hure* – whore (German)

7.

When they finally reached the edge of the rocky cliff and stopped to rest, they found themselves looking at an almost flat hillside covered with small twisted pine trees. After the wet, gloomy ravine, it appeared incredibly open and spacious, with a vast valley stretching far below them, backed by other mountain ranges, which were basking in a pale-blue haze.

"*Genug!*"" she panted. "A little *genug!*"

He silently sat on the edge of a stone slab protruding from the ground. She glanced at the continuous mass of mountains towering above her and then let her eyes linger on the woody downslope, which was speckled with patches of brown earth. Looking upwards, Ivan saw the girl freeze with one foot tucked under her as something caught her gaze like a magnet. Immediately alarmed by the sight, Ivan rose and peered into the distance. The light curves of footpaths glistened here and there in open spaces among pine trees. That meant new trouble. He looked again, and then she grabbed him by the sleeve and started shaking it and speaking with either dismay or hope, without turning to face him, "*Russo, Mensch*"", man!"

------

*   *Genug!* – enough! (German)

**   *Mensch* – person (German)

He had already seen for himself that a man was climbing a path at a measured pace.

They immediately crouched. Forgetting her grudge, she looked inquiringly at him with her dark eyes, while he turned away his frowning face and drew the Browning from beneath his coat. The girl probably understood his intention. Without any explanations, Ivan squeezed her shoulder, indicating that she should stay put, hunched, slipped into a sparse pine forest, and hurried down the slope, hoping to come across the path and parting lower branches along the way.

However, it turned out to be much farther than he had expected.

Choosing places that had a little more trees, he walked quite far away from the ravine and started to regret that he had left her alone. The air was rich with the aroma of conifers, the forest was quiet. However sore his feet had been before, the stones and needles on the ground now turned them into raw flesh. The bright morning sun soon slid from behind the nearby mountain ridge and began to warm up the air. Recalling the previous day, he clicked the release on the plastic grip of his Browning and pulled out the magazine. There were five cartridges inside it, the sixth one was in the barrel. A little reassured, he thought that they might now be lucky enough to come by some clothes and maybe even shoes and food. He was still very hungry, his body was quickly weakening, and the thought of food filled his mouth with saliva, which was coming almost too fast for him to swallow.

All of a sudden, the path slipped into view among the pine trees ten steps ahead. Ivan immediately stopped and looked up and down the slope, but saw no one. As he stood, straining his ears, a little bobtailed bird flitted from under a crooked pine tree next to him, an old cone fell on the ground in the distance, and then everything became perfectly still again. He searched for some cover with his eyes, took a few steps and lowered himself on the prickles and sparse grass behind a mossy fragment of a rock.

He lay prone on the ground and waited, frequently looking downhill at a glistening turn in the path among the treetops. He had no doubt that the man walking there was a civilian, that he would give away his clothes without resistance—after all, Ivan had a gun. But what should he do next? While his conscience would not allow him to kill an unarmed person, it would be almost suicidal to let him pass. No matter how he racked his tired brain, he could not think of anything and felt very bad about his indecision. It was obvious, however, that they would not be able to cross the main ridge without robbing that man.

He turned out to be much closer than Ivan had imagined. Hunching his shoulders under some burden, the man appeared on the path quite suddenly. For some reason, instead of walking, he was almost running, tired and out of breath, casting his eyes around the forest and looking back from time to time. Could he have seen them? Ivan curled up behind the stone as tightly as he could to keep his striped figure out of sight. He cursed under his breath with unexpected anger, disgusted and ashamed of what he had to do.

However, that was necessary.

Ivan let the man come closer, drawing up his legs slowly and turning behind the stone. He felt an ant stirring in his sleeve and stinging like a nettle. Heaving under the weight of his canvas backpack, the Austrian was hurriedly walking along the path in his coarse boots with enormously thick soles. He had almost passed by when Ivan rose and jumped onto the path. The stranger heard him at once and turned around. He was a stocky, even fat man of about sixty, wearing a short leather jacket, a green Tyrolean hat with a badger brush, and frayed trousers baggy at the knees. The Austrian blinked in surprise, swung his arms and started saying something very rapidly in German as he moved towards Ivan. Ivan raised his pistol.

"*Wozu die Pistole?*[*] *Herr Häftling!*[**] *Herr Häftling!*" the Austrian babbled. "*SS!*"

Ivan instantly tensed. He had understood the Austrian but did not want to believe that they were in trouble again. The damned ant was already on patrol between his shoulder blades, but he never tried to shake it off. He was pinning the Austrian with his stern, intense gaze.

"*SS! Dort SS! Streife!*[***]" the man repeated. He was agitated, sweat was streaming down his aged, puffy face, and his chest was wheezing and whistling in every tune like an accordion.

Ivan looked around and bit his lip.

"Where is SS?"

"*Dort! Dort! Ich möchte Ihnen gut machen*[****]," the Austrian was gesticulating with one hand and holding his pack with the other.

---

[*]   *Wozu die Pistole?* – why the pistol? (German)

[**]   *Herr Häftling!* – Mr Prisoner! (German)

[***]   *Dort SS! Streife!* – the SS is over there! Search party! (German)

[****]   *Ich möchte Ihnen gut machen* – I'd like to do something good for you (German)

"*Du nein lügen?*"[*]

"*Nein, nein! Ich bin guter Mensch!*"[**] he said adamantly and, changing his tone, added in broken Russian, "I was prison Sibir."

Something warm briefly lit up in his aged eyes, and Ivan realised that he was not lying. However, they were too exposed and short of time, and that man was their last chance of finding food.

"*Du wer? Warum hier?*"[***] Ivan asked in a stern voice and pulled him unceremoniously away from the path by a jacket sleeve.

"*Ich bin Förster. Dort ist mein Waldhütte*[****]."

Ivan tilted his head back to look in that direction, but saw no cabin. Instead, he saw Giulia burst out of the thicket. She must have heard their conversation, for she now pleaded, "*Russo! Russo!* Run! *Russo.*"

Paying no attention to her cries, Ivan grabbed the Austrian by the shoulder again and pulled forcefully at the pack in his hands. "*Essen?*"[*****]

"*Oh, ja, ja,*" he agreed. "*Brot.*"[******]

By now the Austrian had probably understood everything. He looked around, slipped to his knees, and unzipped the pack with his twitching hands. Ivan reached

---

[*]   *Du nein lügen?* – you no lie? (German)

[**]   *Nein, nein! Ich bin guter Mensch!* – No, no! I'm a good person! (German)

[***]   *Du wer? Warum hier?* – Who you? Why here? (German)

[****]   *Ich bin Förster. Dort ist mein Waldhütte* – I am a forest warden. My cabin is over there (German)

[*****]   *Essen?* – food? (German)

[******]   *Brot* – bread (German)

into the bag and immediately felt a coarse crust of bread under his fingers. He yanked out a small loaf which had already hardened. The Austrian did not protest, but his liveliness was suddenly gone, and Ivan felt a twinge of guilt. However, he immediately stifled that feeling, tightened his jaw and dashed towards the pine trees. Without thinking, he cast a look at the snowy peaks and then glanced over his shoulder. The Austrian was tying up the bag, but something had made his fingers too clumsy to handle the zipper. Ivan threw the bread to Giulia and ran back to the man.

"Take it off!"

He had forgotten the German word for "jacket." The Austrian did not understand his order, so Ivan pulled him by the sleeve to make it clear. However, the Austrian was in no hurry to give away his garment. A look of confusion crossed his aged face.

Ivan shouted, "*Schneller!*" and pulled harder.

"*Schneller! Schneller, Russo!*" Giulia called out of the woods softly but very urgently, and the Austrian took off his jacket with sadness, which suddenly became evident in his every lethargic movement.

Ivan almost tore it out of the man's hands and looked into his eyes for the last time. He knew that they were guilty of base ingratitude and robbery. In the event of failure, the Austrian would also be hanged. But they had no choice.

He ran into the woods where he had just caught a glimpse of Giulia, and then looked over his shoulder—the Austrian was standing at the same place with braces over his grey shirt and watching them, arms down.

---

*   *Schneller* – faster (German)

8.

By now it was not that easy to get far away.

In just fifteen minutes they were breathing heavily through their mouths and dripping sweat as their strides shortened to tiny dragging steps. Meanwhile the pine tree forest had given way to a gentle grassy slope. There the tree line probably stopped. Beyond it there were only brownish mossy rocks and jumbled stones. In the distance, a snow-dusted ridge was basking in the sunshine, standing as grey against the sky as the wing of a quail. The terrain grew even steeper and eventually rose to a bare wall of rocks. Ivan saw that the barrier could not be climbed from where they were. And so he turned and skirted this gigantic fence, looking for a suitable shelter. He had great doubts about the Austrian, whose actions were now impossible to predict. *Anything but the dogs, anything but the dogs*, Ivan thought, convinced that they would not be able to escape if the Germans got on their trail with dogs.

He continued to run, looking down all the time. The whole woody hillside was now in plain sight—the gloomy ravine, where they had spent the night, the pine forest, and a house near it with a high stone gable and galleries along the walls—probably the forester's cabin. He was expecting to see a motorcycle and the Germans there, but they seemed to be running late, and the place looked desolate and empty. The forester was nowhere to be seen either. Tired and confused, he was probably still climbing. During those short, tense minutes, Ivan wished terrible misfortune on those who had forced him to do such a thing. Was he a robber, a villain, why would he have stopped that peaceful fat man and pointed a pistol at him, let alone stolen from him, if it had not been for Nazism, for the war, for the captivity with thousands of tortures and indignities visited on people by the Nazis? They had forced him to commit that robbery, and he hated them all the more.

Threading their way among huge stones on the grassy ground, they reached the top of the hill and saw a ravine, a narrow crack in the wall that lay just within their reach and led inside that fortress of stone. He thought with a sudden joy that they would be able to confuse the dogs if there was a stream in the ravine. In any event, they needed some shelter, for the Germans could catch up with them at any second. Gathering what little strength he had left, Ivan dashed through the grass, and Giulia ran behind him, persevering despite her exhaustion and fear.

Soon they found themselves inside the ravine, with scratches from rhododendron shrubs on their feet. Unfortunately, there was no stream there, only dank, stuffy darkness. Thorny shrubs protruded from the steep stony walls, tufts of coarse grass grew in cracks and among stones, and old bones lay scattered on the ground. Startled by the humans, some night bird snorted and darted deeper into the crack. Although the ravine felt very uncomfortable, Ivan felt a little relieved that they had managed to reach it and hide. He stopped, climbed a tilting mossy stone slab and waited for Giulia. The girl was walking on the stones towards him, swinging one arm for balance. Her short black hair was tousled, her face was bright red with exertion and agitation. But when she looked at Ivan, he saw confusion, fatigue and pain in her eyes, not her usual playfulness.

"*Porca miseria!*[*] We escape, *non?*"

"I wish we had," he replied impatiently. "Hurry up!"

"*Was ist* hurry?" the girl asked.

He did not reply. Breathing heavily, Giulia climbed over to Ivan, and they began walking together.

"Much *gut Vater*[**]! *Communisto Vater,*" she said joyfully.

"A Communist? Hell, no," Ivan said in frustration. "Just a man."

"*Sì, sì,* man, *bene*[***] man," the girl agreed, now a step ahead of him.

He was listening to the faint sounds coming from below, but his eyes were glued to the loaf tucked under her arm. With some sixth sense, Giulia felt his gaze and looked back.

"*Essen!* Bread, no?"

She quickly broke off one edge of the bread crust and held it out to him. Ivan took the crust without hesitation and swallowed it greedily. They had to run and hide, the Germans could appear behind them at any moment, but Ivan could no longer think about anything but the bread. And Giulia understood his silent stillness, for she stopped, crouched, pressing the loaf to her chest, broke off a larger piece with her swift fingers and helpfully shoved it into his large, rough palms. Cupping her hands, she thriftily collected the crumbs that had fallen onto her coat flap and dropped them into her mouth.

---

[*]   *Porca miseria!* – damn! (Italian)

[**]   *Vater* – father (German)

[***]   *Bene* – good (Italian)

Ivan took the bread carefully, turned it around in his hands, seemingly examining it, stole a look at the loaf in her hands from under his brow and slowly started breaking the crust into two. Weighing it with his hands, he held out one half to her. She smiled and quickly took it.

"*Grazie! Non.* Tank you!"

Chewing methodically, he made no response to her expression of gratitude.

They resumed their climb, and the girl also started chewing in silence. Unfortunately, bread was in very short supply and made their hunger only worse. Giulia soon stopped and spun around towards her companion.

"*Russo!* Let's everyting *mangiare*! Accordo,* no?"

Her eyes narrowed and lit up to regain their waywardly playful expression, her fingers squeezed the ragged loaf, ready to tear it apart. Ivan panicked, feeling that their supply, meager to say the least, would be reduced to crumbs.

He lunged towards the girl and grabbed her by the hands. "Give it to me!"

Giulia raised her brow in surprise, and Ivan snatched the bread out of her hands and hurriedly wrapped his leather jacket around it. After her initial confusion, the girl burst out laughing.

He gave her a puzzled look.

"What is it?"

"*Russo* right. Non trust *Brot* Giulia. Word trust, love trust. *Non* trust *Brot* Giulia. *Giusto*—right, *Russo!*"

Still laughing with her eyes, she approached Ivan from behind and touched her palm lightly to his skinny shoulder

------

*   *Mangiare* – eat (Italian)

blade. He hunched his shoulders in embarrassment at her unexpected tenderness.

"Oh, stop it," Ivan muttered. He was about to take a bigger stride when a resonant rifle shot thundered in the distance behind him.

Both of them immediately looked back and froze. Standing on a stone, they heard shouts coming from the general direction of the cabin, immediately followed by the rattle of *Schmeissers** and booming, sputtering echoes over the ravine. Ivan tensed, held his breath, and listened as hard as he could. Their lives now depended on whether they would hear that familiar hateful barking in that mayhem. Fortunately, there seemed to be no dogs within his earshot. Ivan was a little surprised that the bullets were whizzing off to his side, not reaching the ravine. He listened for half a minute, and then a guess flashed through his mind. Shaking off his numbness, Ivan threw the jacket under the girl's feet and scrambled towards the top of the rock, using projections, cracks and shrubs to aid himself.

Bursts of gunfire were rattling and hissing, bullets were zinging over their heads, the distant crackle of motorcycles became discernible in the rumble of shooting. Tilting back her head, Giulia was listening intently and watching Ivan, who had already climbed nearly half the height of the steep rock. He looked back at the entrance to the ravine, climbed a little higher and then froze and lowered his head at the sight of the house and Germans in the distance. Giulia must have guessed what had caught his eye, for she adjusted the jacket, threw off the clogs and shouted something. Although Ivan could see only a small piece of the action near the cabin,

---

*   *Schmeisser* – German machine gun

he was clinging to the rock like glue, unable to take his eyes off that strange scene.

Three motorcyclists were milling around the sparsely wooded grassy area that overlooked the cabin, their machine guns firing into the air in rapid bursts. Several other motorcycles were crackling nearby, apparently trying to get to the rocks, but the drivers were screened from view by a ledge. What seemed to be quite certain was that the Germans had focused their fire and all their attention on someone outside the ravine. The intensity of the fire indicated that they could see the target. Keeping his guess to himself, Ivan took a small sideways step and climbed higher. Hidden by the ledge, he saw a scene that put all his questions to rest.

Giulia was saying something, but he was not listening to her. Gripping the stone ledge with his fingers, he was watching a man in a striped uniform running towards the rocky wall along the slope, taking long strides with his spindly legs. Bullets were smoking and sizzling all around him. The *Häftling* would fall and then jump to his feet and run, only to fall a few seconds later. Two Germans abandoned their motorcycles and were jogging uphill after the fugitive. They were still rather far behind, near the cabin, but others were firing stationary machine guns over their heads. The fire was very heavy and well coordinated, but the *Häftling* pressed on. He occasionally looked back and even seemed to shout something, then fell, and Ivan thought every time that he would not get up. But he was wrong. As soon as the shooting subsided a little, the poor man bounced back to his feet and ran, ran without stopping.

"*Russo! Russo!* What you looking? *Russo!*" Giulia probed, stamping an impatient foot on the stone.

Ivan was watching the wretched man from the rock, afraid to make the slightest move, assuming that his fate had already been sealed. Indeed, the man had almost reached the rock when he fell again and was seen no more. The gunfire immediately ceased.

Ivan's heart sank. He hurried down the stones, carrying with him a quiet sorrow and a glimmer of gratitude for one more defiant death, which had kept the Germans away from that ravine. At last, he jumped to the ground and blurted the news to Giulia, "*Kaputt**."

"*Kaputt?*" she opened her eyes wide in puzzlement.

"Your *compagno***."

"*Krank Häftling?*"

"Yes."

"Uh-oh!"

He snatched his jacket from the confused Giulia. Without saying anything, she grabbed her clogs, and they both rushed uphill.

---

*   *Kaputt* – finished (German)

**   *Compagno* – comrade (Italian)

9.

They had failed to maintain stealth, revealed themselves, left behind a witness, and anxiety gripped Ivan with even greater force—will the Austrian report them or not?

After three attempts to escape, he was experienced enough to know that that was the riskiest situation for fugitives. Nowhere else—in the field or in the mountains—was it easier to fall into a trap than when they visited villages, farmsteads and hamlets and met people. As it happened, even the mistrustful were betrayed, even the careful ran into ambushes. That was often the end of the very difficult road to freedom and the beginning of the agonizing westward march back into captivity. And yet, it was impossible to avoid people altogether. They needed to eat, get directions and change their clothes. There was never any guarantee against betrayal, and fugitives often counted on a lucky coincidence, on human empathy. Many of them were lucky. But not all.

A year ago, he also hoped to scrape through, and he did for thirty-two days. Everything went rather well as the four of them avoided ambushes, swam across rivers, bypassed villages and eluded *Polizeis*[*]. On two occasions, they escaped pursuit. And although they lost Valery, a tank driver from

---

[*]   *Polizei* – [in the occupied territories] locally recruited auxiliary police (German)

Moscow, the other three men stayed out of harm's way and reached their native land, their Volyn. There were Ukrainian villages all around them, peasants were ploughing their strips of land with horses and oxen. The weather was getting warmer. They could sleep in the forest without being chilled to the marrow and mostly stay away from villages. If only they never got hungry! Hunger sometimes forced them to visit villages, and that morning, it was Ivan who went to a village, leaving his mates near a forest. The others had run that errand before, it was now his turn.

It was a little late in the morning when he left the forest and the winding path they had followed all night. Having to settle for the day, they were very reluctant to hide in some hole with empty stomachs. From the edge of the forest, he took a good look at the hamlet but noticed nothing suspicious. There was no big road anywhere in sight, and he headed for the nearest cottage, keeping closer to the shrubs as he crossed a marshy patch. Beneath his coat, Ivan carried a German assault rifle with twelve cartridges he had come by near Krakow. With army boots on his feet and some plain peasant shirt over his shoulders, he looked like everybody else there—an ordinary villager. He reached the vegetable gardens without incident and then made his way from the threshing floor to the nearby cottage along a side path lined by wicker fences. Unfortunately, the house was on the other side of the street. Ivan looked around but saw nobody. He only heard the creaking of a door in the yard and the mooing of a cow—the mistress of the house was probably about to milk it. However, no sooner had he hopped over the road dust—which had settled overnight and was studded with dew—than someone came out of a neighbouring yard. Ivan did not look over his shoulder but felt with the back of his head that he had been spotted. He ducked his head and dashed into the yard. From behind the corner of the house, he finally glanced back. He saw no one, but the canvas trailer of a lorry in the yard across the street caught his eye. The coincidence was unlucky to say the least. To make things even worse, he heard a shout that might have been an order to him or a warning to someone else. Ivan had nowhere to go—a broad harrowed vegetable garden lay beyond the cottage—and he rushed towards the open door of the *sentsy** . At that moment, an unshaven middle-aged man appeared on the threshold. The man must have understood everything without words, for he paled, looked at the assault rifle protruding from Ivan's coat and stepped out of his way back to a doorpost. Without saying anything either, Ivan jumped into the clean, tidy *sentsy* strewn with sweet flag, flicked his eyes back and forth, looking for some cover and, finding nothing suitable, raced through the open door into another room, where the woodstove stood. He spotted a black empty space under the stove, dropped to his knees, and glanced back at the window and benches under it in the icon corner. They were covered with a striped homemade blanket, and three pairs of children's feet stuck out of it. A sense of foreboding gripped him—no, he should not have come there.

But there was no time to change his mind. Boots pounded in the yard, and he climbed backwards into the stinky narrow space under the stove, pressed his side against the wall, squeezed behind the ledge, and tensed. People were already entering the *sentsy*. Ivan had barely stilled his breath when he heard the voices of two or more Germans. The master did not understand or, maybe, did not want to

---

*   *Sentsy* – entryway into a peasant cottage (Belarusian)

understand them. As for Ivan, he could hear everything and needed no interpreter.

"*Wer ist? Wer lief?**" one German was shouting.

"*In diesem Augenblick, ich habe gesehen***," the other one was saying.

"Sirs, I don't understand. There's no one here. I swear!"

Ivan's tension eased slightly. The master was probably their man, he would not betray them. Thank God, Ivan had not been entirely unlucky. All he had to do now was hunker down, wedge himself into the darkest corner so that he would not be found. And so he clung to the wall as tightly as he could, doubled over and almost breathless. Meanwhile, the Germans shouted more loudly and cursed, and the little children in the icon corner began to cry. There was a thud as a woman who must have been sitting on the stove jumped to the floor. She rushed towards the children and began to comfort them. Someone ran into the cottage and snapped the bolt of an assault rifle. A shadow darted across the bottom of the stove. The children's crying grew louder, the couches groaned—the intruders were stripping their beds. Ivan waited, keeping his hand on the butt of the assault rifle, knowing full well that he could not fire it there. Boots stomped, and the Germans apparently went on to examine the top of the stove. The metal door of the stove clanked, and a flashlight beam immediately flickered on the wall behind him. He squinted instinctively, expecting them to shout, "*Herauskriechen!****" But the beam was a little

---

*   *Wer ist? Wer lief?* – Who is it? Who was running? (German)

**   *In diesem Augenblick, ich habe gesehen* – I have just this moment seen (German)

***   *Herauskriechen!* – out you crawl! (German)

dim—the battery must have run low—the Germans noticed nothing and the tramp of boots resumed. The footfalls soon faded—they were probably searching the *sentsy*. Not daring to move yet, he exhaled and then slowly inhaled, heartened but confused. Had he really escaped? Indeed, the footfalls died away. Only the children were snuffling near the stove, and the mother's bare heels were slapping on the floor as she darted from window to window—sounds of German conversation were now coming from the yard. The master was saying something, apparently trying to distract them from the house. Indeed, all noises soon ceased, the man must have entered the *sentsy*, and his wife joined him. She started talking very rapidly, whimpering and almost crying. "Enough of this! Calm down!" the master snapped. She fell silent, returned to the house and began cooing over the children.

Ivan had already begun to wonder whether it was time to get out and find some good shelter when the woman cried out in terror, "Petro, Petro! God help us! Hryts is coming."

Ivan tensed again. The master disappeared somewhere for about a minute. Then he heard an indulgent and sarcastic voice in the yard, "Good day to you, Herr Petro!" The master stiffly returned the greeting, Ivan heard something like the crack of a whip on a leather boot, and the same person said in an oddly casual voice, as if he was talking about a dog or a kitten.

"Who are you hiding? Bring him over now!"

"I'm not hiding anyone, *kum** Hryts! Cross my heart. What are you talking about?"

"Of course you're not. All right, let's check. Hanna!" Hryts shouted.

---

*   *Kum* – godfather of a child

"I'm here, *kum*," replied the frightened woman, who was standing in the doorway.

"Who is Petro hiding? Confess!"

"Oh, how could I possibly know? He isn't hiding anyone, *kum* Hryts."

"No, he isn't. Come on, Nastusya, tell me, where is your daddy hiding the bandit?"

"I don't know" said a frightened child's voice.

"Don't know? We'll see," Hryts said with a sinister calmness.

Ivan's cheekbones froze in a rictus of anger. He wanted so badly to get out of that hole and pump a dozen bullets into that monster's gut. However, Ivan did not know how many helpers he had. He thought with a sinking feeling that Hryts knew his job well, he was not a German.

"Hlukh, bring me some straw. You go too, Zhupan. We'll soon find out where he is hiding. We'll grill him."

There was a rush of feet in the yard and the clanging of what must have been the barn door. Ivan understood what that Hryts was up to, the devil take him. *But would they dare set the place on fire, would they do this to one of their own, who even calls this monster 'kum'?* Ivan thought in horror.

Meanwhile, something rustled near the windows and obscured the light under the stove. *They must have put in the straw,* Ivan thought. Then everything grew quiet, and there were no longer any footfalls or conversation. Suddenly, a woman began to scream. It was as if she and not her house was being burnt, so desperate and wild was her voice. Hearing her sobs, all the children began to wail too, and Ivan immediately smelled smoke. He thought that everything had been lost, that he would not only burn himself to death but also cause other people to die. He probably ought to have got out and shot that swine dead, but he still had a glimmer of hope that they would not let the building catch fire and were merely trying to scare him.

But then, would it not be too much misery for the man and his family if Ivan allowed the house to catch fire and then climbed out? He realised that a decision had to be made in seconds but simply did not know what to do.

He would probably have jumped out from under the stove—he was already poised for a jump—if it had not been for the woman bursting into the house all of a sudden with wailing and curses. Before he realised what she was doing, she stamped her feet near the stove, bent over and cried between sobs, "Get out! Get out! The house is being burnt because of you. Beast! What wind blew you here? Get out!"

Ivan could not help a sigh of relief that everything was over, however unexpectedly. He shoved the assault rifle under the litter in the corner and climbed out. He was not angry with the woman, just very sad and sorry that his long and arduous journey had come to such a silly end.

And so he stepped on to the threshold, calm and ready for anything. Four young men in the yard were glowering at him. One of them stood out—a real hunk wearing light cotton trousers and a blue arm band. He was probably that Hryts. The man was holding a cocked gun—a Russian carbine, Ivan could tell by its bolt. He thought at that moment that they would not dare kill him there. They had to hand him over to the Germans.

And so they did.

10.

Stifling his shivery anxiety, Ivan was looking around and listening, afraid that the Germans would let their dogs loose. However, time was going by, and everything around them remained quiet. Finally he concluded that the Austrian had not reported them after all, and the motorcyclists had probably not found their tracks and left the fugitives alone for a while. Besides, they had collected the dead body of the mad *Häftling* and would not return to the camp empty-handed. As he pondered his situation, Ivan's anxious agitation gradually gave way to other thoughts and worries.

The ravine gradually narrowed as it wound its way higher and higher into the mountains, like a twisty corridor with gigantic walls. They had followed it for at least four hours almost without stopping. The air grew chilly and damp. Falling pressure felt like cotton wool in their ears, slowly muffling all sounds. The sun was rising, but its light never reached the ravine. Shrouded by the clouds, the radiant blue sky finally disappeared. Patches of blue-grey fog were sailing swiftly over the ravine, catching on the tops of the rocks. A wind began to blow in strong gusts, and the temperature dropped so steeply that walking no longer did much to keep them warm. They could not look around to see how far they were from the town, but Ivan felt that they had to be on high ground, why else would they be so cold? Even so, he did not put on the leather jacket with the bread wrapped in it. He knew that the worst still lay ahead, that it would get even colder, and that they might have to walk through snow. As a matter of fact, he worried little about himself—he could walk even faster. Although he was tired and his feet had been bruised by the stones, he was capable of more. How many times Ivan had already been saved by his great natural strength, ability to live in any conditions, and, of course, his rigorous army training! How many times he had endured while others had run out of steam, fallen and stopped because of hunger, fatigue and sleepless nights both on the front and in captivity! He was already beginning to think that that trial would be no exception, that he would somehow endure it and get over the ridge—how could he not? As long as he was alive, he would put up and cope with anything. Freedom is always better than captivity.

If only it had not been for Giulia.

Although she was obviously working hard and almost keeping pace with him, he stopped from time to time and eyed her with suspicion and wariness. Keenly aware of his attention, the girl smiled weakly every time, trying to pretend that she was fine, unafraid and still strong. However, her slow movements, so out of keeping with her impetuous temperament, indicated more eloquently than words that she was very tired.

At some point, after rounding another corner, they found themselves at the end of the tapering ravine. A steep rock blocked their path like a dam about a hundred steps away. However reluctant they were to leave their shelter, they had to climb out to face the wind on the exposed bare rocks. There was probably a way to go from there.

Ivan walked towards the steep incline, then began to climb. Near the top, he dropped to one knee and waited for

Giulia. She was climbing a little more slowly, too tired to keep her head up. Ivan braced himself with his extended leg and gave her his hand. The girl grabbed it with her soft, cold fingers. Without looking back any more, he dragged her up.

They climbed out of the ravine and found themselves on a bare slope that was covered with stones but not very steep. However, they did not have time to look around. A gust of wind punched them hard in their chests, ragged patches of fog descended on the stones, a chilly wetness resembling damp smoke swiftly shrouded the rocks and the sky. The sheet was not entirely solid—brown rocks flashed here and there through breaks in the fog. In the distance, there were bluish gaps. However, it was impossible to discern the landscape through them. And so they stopped, and Giulia immediately leaned her shoulder against a rocky projection. The wind was tearing viciously at their legs and sleeves and ripping at the hems of their coats. It became even colder. Ivan put the brownish leather jacket on the ground, pulled the bread out of the once neat but now worn garment and took a step in her direction with the jacket.

"Oh, *non, non.* No! I warm." Her eyes flicked towards him, brightening again, and her hand flew up. Her close-cropped hair was rippling in the wind.

Without saying anything, Ivan draped the garment over her thin, sharp shoulders. The girl pulled it reluctantly over herself and immediately hunched against the cold and drew in her head. He crouched over the partially eaten loaf of bread. They could probably have one more small meal.

"*Il pane*. Brot!*" she said with hungry impulsiveness, guessing his intention.

---

*   *Pane* – bread (Italian)

To begin with, Ivan examined the bread, held it in his hand, as if to determine its weight and the size of the smallest ration they could afford this time. He sighed—if only the loaf was not so tiny! Giulia lowered herself to the ground and quickly moved over to him. Afraid to lose some crumbs, Ivan did not break it. Instead, he looked back, picked up a sharp piece of stone and carefully started cutting off their portion. Huddled in the leather jacket, the girl was watching his rough hands with a strange tenderness as he cut and then divided the slice in two, broke off bits from one half and added them to the other and then re-examined everything.

"*Gut?*"

"*Sì, sì. Gut.*"

Once again, the cold and their fatigue seemed to disappear. Giulia's eyes shone as she waited impatiently for permission to eat that meagre ration. However, Ivan lingered. With impressive self-control, he broke off some more crumbs. Then he abruptly told the girl, "Turn around."

She understood his intention. Without taking her hands from under the jacket, she quickly turned, and he touched his finger to the piece with some extra crumbs.

"Who's going to have it?"

"*Russo!*" she said with resolute readiness and whirled towards him and the bread.

Without a word, Ivan carefully took the thin slice. She picked up the other one a little faster.

"*Gra...*Tank you, *Russo!*"

"Not at all," Ivan said.

"*Russo!*" Giulia called out to him, chewing hurriedly and wrapping the jacket tighter around herself. "You name Ivan, *non?*"

"Ivan," he confirmed, a little surprised.

Seeing his puzzlement, she tossed her head and laughed.

"Ivan! Giulia guess! How guess?"

"Not difficult to guess."

"All, all *Russo*—Ivan? *Non?*"

"Well, not all. But many. A lot."

Giulia suddenly lost her momentary gaiety. She gave a tired sigh, hunched into the jacket with a shiver, and stole a glance at the loaf on the ground. He was slowly eating his slice, drawing out the pleasure.

Catching her very eloquent glance, Ivan took the loaf to put it under his coat. However, before he could hide it, Giulia gave a little cry of surprise and froze. His head snapped up in alarm—there was fear on the girl's face, her wide open eyes were staring blankly at something over his shoulder. Ivan turned around with the bread in his hand and immediately saw what had frightened her.

In a distant clearing in the fog, a ghastly-looking *Häftling* in a torn coat was sitting on a rock, leaning on his hands. His bare skull and thin neck were sticking out of the wide collar of his striped coat, which bore a red number and a triangle. The *Häftling* was watching them intently through the gaping black holes of his eye sockets. He must have seen the bread in their hands, for he shuddered and began to jump up and down, chanting in a hoarse voice, "*Brot! Brot! Brot!*"

Then he fell silent, shivered and demanded in a voice that now sounded perfectly human but full of despair, "*Gib Brot!*"*

"Huh, some hope," Ivan smiled sarcastically, looking at him.

---

*   *Gib Brot!* – give bread (German)

The *Häftling* lingered for a few seconds, and then shouted with unexpected anger, "*Gib Brot! Gib Brot! Ich bescheine Gestapo**! *Gib Brot!*"

"Ah, *Gestapo!*" Ivan rose to his feet. "Get the hell out of here! Now!"

Ivan started menacingly towards the madman, but after he had taken a few steps, the *Häftling* leapt off the rock and ran downhill.

"*Gib Brot—nichts Gestapo! Nichts Brot—Gestapo!***"

"Damn you, dog!" Ivan shouted into the wind.

Seized by anger, he stepped forward to chase after the blackmailer, but the madman cautiously retreated farther out of reach. He halted when he saw Ivan stop.

"*Gib Brot!*"

Ivan stuck a hand beneath his coat and the German froze, waiting, but Ivan yanked out a pistol and snapped its trigger.

"*Pistole!*" the madman screamed in fear and bolted.

Ivan bit his lip, Giulia jumped over to him from behind.

"Give him *Brot!* Give him *Brot!*" she babbled nervously.

Meanwhile, the madman ran a little farther, stopped and then hurried downhill, looking over his shoulder.

"Ivan give *Brot!* Give *Brot!* Non Gestapo!" the girl demanded fearfully.

A traitorous bastard, Ivan thought, looking angrily at the madman's wobbly figure. *You can't mess with him. He'll make a noise and go to the Germans. What can you do to a madman? You'd feel sorry if you killed him, but you can't get*

---

*   *Ich bescheine Gestapo* – [here intended to mean] I'll inform Gestapo (German)

**   *Gib Brot—nichts Gestapo! Nichts Brot—Gestapo!* – give bread – no Gestapo! No bread – Gestapo! (German) *rid of him either. And then the Germans will come with dogs, they'll pick up the trail, and it's all over.*

"Hey!" Ivan shouted to the madman. "Take *Brot!*"

The *Häftling* clutched at a rock to stop himself, looked back and even seemed to ponder something. Then he shouted over the wind, "*Nichts. Du schiessen*. Ich bescheine Gestapo!* " and continued downhill.

"Go to the devil! *Nicht schiessen.* Here you are. Here." And indeed, Ivan broke off a piece of the loaf and raised it in his hand for the madman to see. Standing nearby, Giulia was shaking from cold and anxiously looking at the *Häftling* anxiously. The man stood for a while, then lowered himself on a rocky projection. He was afraid to approach them.

"Damn you, dog!" Ivan shouted, losing his patience. "To hell with you! Go to the Gestapo! Go!!!"

"Ivan, *non* Gestapo! *Non,* Ivan!" Giulia was jerking his sleeve. "Give little *Brot. Non* Gestapo."

"Like hell he'll get bread. Let him go."

"He bad *Häftling.* He *krank.* He Gestapo."

Ivan did not reply. He put the half of the loaf and the pistol beneath his coat and headed back up the slope. Giulia was walking silently beside him. He felt that it was dangerous to treat the madman like that, but he could not yield now—his angry stubbornness had proven stronger than his prudence. Giulia kept looking back until a mist rolled in and hid everything except the grey jumble of rocks. Everywhere in the distance below and on either side there were rushing, curling, surging tendrils of damp fog. They did not know whether the *Häftling* was sitting there or had really returned. Noticing alarm on the girl's face,

---

*   *Du schiessen* – you shoot

Ivan said, "He won't go anywhere. He's lying through his teeth."

He was calming her, and yet he did not feel calm himself. Human life depends on God knows whom! Where on Earth is justice? Mad as the *Häftling* was, he had survived, found his way into the mountains, dodged pursuers and escaped bullets. Meanwhile, how many of the best lads had fallen in the camp?

Talk about justice, such a rare commodity these days!

They were already on their way, walking around an enormous layered ledge, when Ivan looked over his shoulder and reached beneath his coat. Giulia also looked back, but the madman was nowhere to be seen. Even so, Ivan took out the morsel, returned, and, finding a suitable place, put it on the stone they had recently sat on.

"All right. Let this devil have his way! Let him choke on it!" Ivan mumbled, as if to excuse himself.

Giulia kept silent to signal her approval.

11.

The wind was driving strands of fog in an endless stream. Ivan's coat grew damp, and shivers were going up and down his spine. He was looking back all the time and beginning to doubt that the madman would find the crust. He even felt an urge to return, pick it up and eat it himself. To shake off nagging doubts, he started climbing faster away from that place.

They soon rounded the gigantic layered ledge, which jutted into the sky like a petrified bird's tail, climbed higher, and then the foggy cloud suddenly split and sagged. They saw a steep wall of bare rocks overhead and a path on a slope just a stone's throw away. It ran neither up nor down but gently wound its way among stones, cutting across the slope. Although the path was not that easy to notice amid that chaos of rocks, both immediately saw it, much to their delight.

Ivan was the first to set foot on the trail and look down—bleak rocks and crevasses interspersed with blue-grey colours of the more distant scenery were flashing between wisps of fog. A dappled ridge with a deep snow cover was shining in the misty sky high above them. After a closer look Ivan actually saw two ridges—the more distant one was mighty and broad, resembling the grey motionless back of a bear. The other one was jagged, lightly dusted with snow and edged by a saddle-sided mountain. Its summit touched the sky and appeared to be the tallest one from his vantage point, but Ivan was already familiar with the deceptiveness of the mountains, which makes the nearest peak look like the highest elevation. That distant bear's ridge seemed to be the more important one after all. Their coveted destination—the partisan Trieste—probably lay beyond it.

Ivan stood for a minute with his head tilted back, surveying that barrier in their path to the future, longing for proof that they would not be pursued again, that the worst was already over, that they would not meet any more people, and that nature was now their only adversary and all they needed to fight it was more energy. Then he looked at Giulia, who was subdued now and probably overcome with a new anxiety similar to his. She was fluttering her bushy eyebrows, also peering at the snowy ridges. And then, probably for the first time, he felt a quiet satisfaction that he was not facing the formidable uncertainty of the mountain journey alone, that he was accompanied by another human, even though that was a woman. "*Ayda?*" he offered with a flicker of joy.

However unlikely she was to know that boyish word, their feelings were so much in tune now that she readily echoed, "*Ayda!*""

And so they set out along the path, which spanned the bare, rocky slope like a belt. The sun was already low in the sky, glaring through breaks in the fog. Blindingly white patches of clouds shone over mountain slopes. Black shreds of shadows were racing over the rocks and chasms, juxtaposed by bright patches of light. The unrelenting wind

---

*   *Ayda?* – shall we go? (Belarusian)

**   *Ayda!* – let's go!

was tearing at Ivan's coat, blowing into his trousers through a hole and inflating them like a balloon. Giulia turned up the wide collar of her leather jacket to ward off the chill. They climbed higher. Illuminated by the sun, the black crack of the ravine and rocky hillsides came into clear view in the distance below, as did a feathery outcrop that cast a huge shadow over one of the slopes. Ivan stopped at the sight of the stone they had recently sat on. There was the crazy *Häftling* shuffling along on his thin legs, bent over, seemingly looking for something underfoot.

"How nice. He's following us."

"*Tragico* man," Giulia said. "*Peccato*—pity!"

"Why pity him? Scum."

"He want *Russo* go. But *Russo böse*. He afraid."

"Very wise of him," Ivan noted curtly.

He moved on, ignoring the madman, although not very comfortable about his presence. But what can you do with a lunatic? The fugitives could neither chase him away nor hide themselves anywhere. They probably had to put up with him until the night.

"Ivan," she said, stressing the "i." "You *non* angry Giulia?"

"Why should I be angry?"

"You *non böse?*"

"You may feel safe."

"*Non* afraid, *non?*"

"No."

Tinged by fatigue, her face lost its lenient smiling expression and grew more serious to reflect her sad thoughts.

"Giulia *Russo non* fear. Giulia snow fear."

Ivan, who was walking ahead of her, just sighed in response. He was also more and more concerned about the snow and their meagre supply of bread. He wished they had taken more from the forester. They definitely needed his footwear—how they would walk on the snow barefoot was difficult to imagine. Alas, his bright ideas were always late. Needless to say, they had not been thinking at that moment about the snowy summits. They were happy to slip through the Nazis' dragnet alive. At any rate, they should be grateful to the Austrian. They would have no bread if it had not been for him. Ivan was quickly walking along the path. The setting sun was shining brightly off to his side, but its light was cold. Two shadows were crawling and flashing over the slope, reaching all the way to its bottom. He was unwilling to comfort the girl or reason with her. "You have a coat. There's nothing to fear. There will be no *manto**," he simply said.

Giulia sighed audibly and said after a pause, "*Roma* Giulia much *manto* had. *Vier manto*—black, white."

He pricked up his ears and slowed down.

"Four *mantos?*"

"*Ja. Vier manto.*" "Four," she added.

"Does this mean you're rich?"

She laughed.

"Oh, *non* rich. Poor. *Politische Häftling.*"

"All right, is your father rich? What is your father?"

"*Vater?*"

"Father. Well, your papa. What is he?"

"Ah, *il padre***!" she understood. "*Il padre commerciante. Direttore firma****."

---

*   *Manto* – cloak (Italian)

**   *Padre* – father (Italian)

***   *Il padre commerciante. Direttore firma* – father is a businessman, a company director (Italian)

He whistled softly. How great, she is a bourgeois. *What if her father turns out to be a fascist for good measure? What a nice little walk in the Alps this would be. No one in your camp would ever believe you're innocent,* he thought and abruptly turned around.

"Father fascist?"

"Si, *fascista,*" Giulia replied simply, looking with liveliness into his hardening eyes. "*Milito* chief*."

That is even better! What the hell is going on in this world? As Zhuk put it, throw a stick at a dog, and you will hit a fascist. Shame on Europe!

He stepped aside, letting the girl catch up with him, and examined his slender, long-legged, and shabbily dressed companion with obvious interest. However ridiculous, her motley collection of secondhand clothes could not eclipse her youthful elegance and beauty. They were evident in everything—the flexibility of her movements, the affectionate loveliness of her face, the dignified and graceful turn of her head. She was glancing at him with submission and devotion, her fingers interlocked inside the long sleeves of the jacket, her clumsy clogs making the usual clicking sounds.

"And you? Perhaps you're also a fascist?" Ivan asked with a heightened inner sensitivity to her.

The girl gave him a sharp, quietly reproachful look.

"Giulia *fascista?* Giulia *Comunista!*" she declared with a fully conscious pride.

"You?"

"I!"

---

*   *i.e.* he was a chief of the *Milizia,* a volunteer police force in fascist Italy

"You're lying," he said incredulously after a pause. "What kind of Communist could you be?"

"*Comunista. Si,* Giulia *Comunista.*"

"Did you join the party then? Did you have a card?'"

"Oh, no. *Non la tessera**. Formally *non. Moralmente Comunista.*"

"Ah, morally! Morally doesn't count."

"Why?" He made no reply. What could one say to that naive question? If everyone who calls himself a Communist was counted, how many Communists would there be? In addition, she is a bourgeois. Who would admit her to the party? She is just babbling.

Ivan started walking faster, letting his interest subside a little.

"We count only those who have cards."

"Ah, *Russland! Russland* different. I understand. *Russland sovietica. Russland* freedom."

"Yes, it's not like your bourgeoisdom."

"*Sovietica* very *gut. Emancipazione. Libertà. Fratellanza***. Right?"

"Yes."

"Very *gut*," she said heartily. "Giulia respect *Russland* very, very much. *Non fascismo. Non* Gestapo. Very *gut*. Ivan happy his country, *non?*" She ran up to him and gripped his arm above the elbow with both hands. "Say, Ivan, how live before war? How your village? Listen, *signorini*, girl loved you?" she suddenly asked, looking into his anxious face with a playful devotion.

---

*   *Non la tessera* – no card (Italian)

**   *Emancipazione. Libertà. Fratellanza* – emancipation, liberty, fraternity (Italian)

Ivan blinked in embarrassment but did not withdraw his hand. Her gentle closeness stirred up an unusual warmth within him.

"Nonsense, what girl? We had too much to worry about."

"Why?"

"We just did."

"Your life hard? Why?"

All of a sudden Ivan realised that he had said too much. He did not want to tell her about his life.

"Yes, things happened."

"*Non,* you *non* saying truth," she said, squinting at him with a cunning look in her watchful eyes. "Love many *signorina!*"

"Nonsense!"

"What province you from? Where you live? Moscow, Kyiv?"

"Belarus."

"Belarus. Is it province?"

"Republic."

"*Repubblica?* Dis is *gut. Italia monarchia. Monte, montagne* have in your *repubblica?*"

"No, there're no mountains. We have forests. Rivers and lakes, the most beautiful lakes," he said, yielding to memories in spite of himself. "There're two lakes right near my village, Tsyareshki. Look at them on a quiet evening, and they are absolutely still. Like a mirror. And the forest hanging upside down is like a painting. The only ripples are from the fish. The pike are this big! Your mountains are a joke."

Ivan had said too much in one breath for his reserved personality. Immediately sensing that, he dropped silent. However, his agitated thoughts and fantasies had already taken him back to his distant homeland. And now, in that wild jumble of rocks, he started to feel unbearably lonely, the way he had not felt for a long time in captivity.

She must have sensed that, for she asked when he fell silent, "Speak more, speak Belarus."

A grey hazy cloud shrouded the sun again.

Swift, grey shadows descended on the smooth slope and a trail running across it, moist, smoky wisps scudded over the hill. It was cold and windy.

Not very coherent or eager to talk at first, halting frequently, reliving old experiences like something distant, valuable and extraordinary, he began telling her about oak groves strewn with large acorns, about beaver lodges on forest lakes, about the cool healing birch sap in the spring and about the aroma of blooming bird cherry trees in May.

Ivan had not been so talkative and light-hearted for a long time and could not recognise himself now. And Giulia's attentive interest to the place where he belonged immediately had some endearing effect on him, making him feel as if they had known each other for a long time and had met after a long and difficult period of separation.

Finally he fell silent. She slowly let go of his arm and took his rough fingers, relaxing her grip. Then she asked quietly, "Ivan, your mama *gut?*"

"Mama? *Gut.*"

"And *il padre,* your papa?"

She was looking dreamily at the slope and did not notice his sudden mood change as his face flinched and fell.

"I don't remember."

"Why?" she asked in surprise and even stopped.

He moved on, letting their linked arms stretch.

"Dad died when I was small."

"*Morto?* Die? Why die?"

"A disease killed him."

She carefully released his fingers and took a small step forward to be at his side, expecting him to say something important, explain what she could not understand.

But he no longer wanted to talk about anything and just sighed, thinking that it would probably be better for her not to hear about the difficult and painful episodes of his life.

12.

Those were Ivan's thoughts while he was climbing the steep trail, certain that he was doing the right thing. Indeed, who was she, a pampered beauty, a glittering fragment of the alien, distant world, who had landed in a Nazi camp by a strange quirk of war fate? Who was she that he should reveal to her his pain, the things that had once stolen so much of his inner peace? However good and decent it might be, would the soul of that girl accept the hard truth that was so confusing even to him?

Deep in thought, Ivan was walking briskly, oblivious to time. Giulia must have realised that she had struck a painful chord in his heart, for she stopped talking, fell behind a little and stayed respectfully silent for a long time as they climbed together. Meanwhile, a restless windy evening spread over the chaotic, majestic jumble of rocks. Darkness was rapidly descending on the mountains, making the overcast horizon even narrower. The rippling mist swallowed up what was left of the bright silvery glitter of the distant ridge. The giant twin summits of the other ridge, one slightly taller than the other, stood black against the lighter sky. The trail led to the saddle. There they would probably find a pass.

The evening was the most oppressive time of the day for Ivan. Never—in the day, at night or early in the morning—did he feel so lonely, so ill at ease and sad, as he did at dusk. The feeling became really intense during the war years, especially in captivity, in a strange land, in distress, hunger and cold. Never had he been so acutely aware of his loneliness, helplessness, and dependence on a ruthless hostile force or longed for peace, goodness and the presence of a kindred spirit so desperately.

"Ivan!" Giulia suddenly called out from behind. "Ivan!"

As always, she was stressing the wrong syllable, sounding exotic and even startling him by the suddenness of her call. It was as if someone else had joined the two of them.

Ivan stopped abruptly.

Saying nothing else, Giulia was plodding along among the stones. It was clear even without words how tired the girl was. Ivan, too, felt how badly he needed rest, but it was unbearably cold at that soaring height. The wind was raging, ripping at their clothes and howling in the ravines. Their hands got very cold as they walked, and their feet went completely numb. Meanwhile the temperature kept dropping, and the wind was growing stronger as night approached. Nature was bringing all its brute, blind force to bear on those two humans. Ivan was in a great hurry, knowing full well that they could not spend the night there, that walking was their only salvation, and it would be too late tomorrow if they did not cross the mountains by the morning.

"Ivan," Giulia said, coming closer. "Very, very tired."

He shifted from foot to foot, the soles of his feet were aching, stinging, throbbing from cold, but he was paying no attention to his pain. He was anxiously looking at Giulia.

"Hang in there. See, the weather is getting worse."

A thick dark cloud was heaving its bulk over the twin summits and settling on the slopes. The sky was slowly fading to black. A tiny solitary star twinkled dimly and vanished behind the black veil. A murky mishmash of clouds shrouded the greying landscape—the rocky mounds, slopes, and ravines.

"Why *non* pass? Where *ist* pass?"

"It's close. Close," Ivan reassured the girl, not knowing himself how far that saddle was.

Once again they found themselves walking along a trail that was barely visible on the stony ground. After a while Ivan began to worry that he would lose it. He kept climbing at a measured pace, listening to the familiar tapping of Giulia's clogs. Where the slope was really steep, he stopped, waited for the girl, gave her his hand and dragged her up, barely keeping his heartbeat in check.

And the wind was ripping madly at their clothes, punching them hard in the back and chest, taking their breath away, whirling among stones, frequently changing direction—they could not even tell where the gusts were coming from.

Meanwhile, the darkness became complete, the towering rocks blended into one impenetrable mass, the sky and the mountains formed a single pitch-black expanse. It was so dark that Ivan began to stumble and trip over stones and bruised his legs several times. It was at that point that he felt the first jolt of anxiety—where was the trail? Bending over for a closer look and running his hands over a piece of debris, he realised that the path was gone—they had lost their way.

And so he stopped, turned away from the wind, and tensed all his muscles, waiting for the girl. "Wait here!" Ivan said sharply when her exhausted figure finally reached him. He stepped aside, peering at the ground. Silent and almost indifferent to him, she immediately slumped on a stone and hunched against the wind. Stifling his anxiety, Ivan walked a little farther, darted back and forth, examining the ground and occasionally probing it with his feet. The trail was gone. Little by little, he began to notice some blinking, slanting shapes in the surrounding darkness and put out his hand—it was snowing. Sparse, fine dust was driving sideways from the windy black abyss, bouncing on stones, gathering in small pits and cracks and on the ground. Ivan stayed put for a little longer, looking around and dithering. The snow became thicker and the grey mixture of stains made the ground a little lighter. And then he noticed the white curve of the trail not far away.

"Hey, Giulia!" he called softly.

The girl did not reply. He waited a little longer, battling frustration. *Is she asleep or something? What a nice companion! Good for nothing but garden walks.*

The wind was still raging, snow grains were flashing, rustling over stones, a nagging pain was developing in his feet. His hands were hidden in his sleeves. The Browning beneath his coat was stinging his skin with its slippery cold surface.

"Hey, Giulia!"

Once again she gave no reply. Cursing under his breath, Ivan reluctantly walked back where he had left her, making his way gingerly over the wet, cold stones.

Giulia was sitting on the stone, doubled up, with her leather coat draped over her body and even covering her knees. She was as silent as she had been the previous night and did not raise her head when he approached her. Ivan stopped and stood over her in confusion and dismay.

"*Basta**, Ivan," she said softly without lifting her head.

He kept silent.

"What do you mean *'basta'*? Get up, now!"

"*Non* get up. No get up."

"Are you joking?"

No reply.

"Stand up I say! We're almost there. Your feet will run on their own on the way down."

No reply.

"Hey, can you hear me?"

"*Finito. Non* Giulia march. *Non.*"

"You see, we cannot stop here. We'll freeze to death. Look at the snow."

Alas, his words were having no impact on her. He saw how exhausted she was and felt the powerlessness of his logic. But how could he force her to go? After a little thought he reached beneath his coat, pulled out the crumbled loaf and, turning away from the wind, carefully broke off a tiny piece.

"Take some bread. Eat!"

"*Brot?*"

She seemed to perk up and immediately raised her head. Ivan shoved the bread into her hands, and she ate it in a few bites.

"More *Brot?*"

"No, I won't give you more."

"Little, little *Brot.* Give *Brot!*" she asked like a wayward child.

"I'll give you more at the pass."

All at once, her form went limp on the dark ground, and she was still.

———————————

*   *Basta* – enough (Italian)

"*Non* pass."

"To hell with your *nons!*" he suddenly exploded, standing opposite her. "Get up at once. What do you want? Freeze to death? Who would you harm? The Germans? Or do you want to do them a service and return to the camp? Oh yeah, they're waiting. You'll show them where Ivan has gone!" he shouted, choking from strong gusts of wind.

She threw up her head without changing her posture. "*Non* camp."

"You won't go to the camp? Where will you go then?"

She said nothing in reply, dropped her head again and curled into a small living ball.

"Come on, you'll freeze to death! You silly little thing! You'll be finished by the morning," he said, softening a little.

She kept silent.

The wind continued to drive snow. The snowflakes were sparse and small, but the landscape gradually lightened up. Greyish holes opened everywhere in the blackness of the night, and visibility improved. However, their motionless bodies were now rapidly losing heat and shivering from cold.

"Get up immediately!" Ivan yanked her by the coat and ordered in a stern military voice, "To your feet!"

After a pause, she struggled up, took the first step in her clogs and slowly plodded after him, clutching at stones and swaying weakly in the wind gusts. With a frown on his face, Ivan was shuffling towards the trail. He was already beginning to hope that things would somehow work themselves out, that she would hit her stride. He knew that the worst thing in her condition was to lose pace, even sit down—if she did, it would be extremely difficult for her to get back on her feet. They were approaching the trail when a strong gust of wind lashed across their faces with a dash of snow and hit them in the chest, taking their breath away and knocking Giulia to the ground.

He tried to help her up at first, took her hand, but Giulia would not get up. She began to cough, then struggled to catch her breath. At long last, she sat up and announced with the calm resolve of a person who had made a final decision, "Giulia *finito. Alles*[*]. Ivan Trieste. Giulia *non* Trieste. *Alles non.*"

"Out of the question."

He stepped aside and also sat on a rocky projection.

"And this is someone who called herself a Communist," he said reproachfully. "An alarmist, that's who you are."

"Giulia non *alarmista,*" the girl bristled. "Giulia *partigiano*[**]."

Noticing the hurt in her voice, Ivan decided to use it to his own advantage. *Maybe this will stir her up,* he thought.

"An alarmist, who else could you be?"

"Giulia *non alarmista.* Little *energia.*"

"Then just force yourself," he said more quietly. "I'll tell you a story from the front. From the *Ostfront,* where you were headed. We're in a house surrounded by Krauts. No one can get out. Assault rifles are firing at the windows, the Germans are shouting, 'Rus, surrender!' So our platoon commander also says, '*Alles. Kaputt.*' And then company commander Belasheyew yells , 'Stop! That's not why we have guns! Let's fight our way out.' And so all of us jump into the doorway with all our assault rifles blazing, and then dive under the fence and behind the corners. And

------

[*]   *finito. Alles* – finished. It's all over (Italian and German)

[**]   *Partigiano* – partisan (Italian)

guess what, we did break free. Of course, five of us died. Belasheyew too. But four survived."

Giulia kept silent.

"So, shall we go?"

No reply.

"Why the hell don't you say anything?" He was shivering with cold and beginning to lose his patience. "You'll freeze to death, you silly girl. What was the point of escaping, climbing all the way to the sky?"

She kept silent.

"And what did the lads die for when they blew up that bomb? So that at least someone would survive, but you've just fallen to pieces, haven't you?"

He jumped to his feet and started walking up and down the trail, feeling that the wind had chilled him to the marrow. His bare feet left faint prints on the grey ground. They were lucky that it was not freezing cold, but the temperature was probably going to fall in the predawn hours, and then they would both die there. Ivan stopped resolutely next to Giulia.

"So, you're not coming?"

"*Non*, Ivan."

"All right, do as you wish. Die," he said with deliberate indifference and ordered grimly, "Give me the clogs!"

She stirred weakly, took off the clogs and put one foot on the other to keep it from the cold. He immediately thrust his numb feet into those unsightly shoes, which still retained her warmth.

"Throw off the jacket, too."

She removed it obediently. Although a little too broad at the shoulders, Ivan pulled the jacket on without hesitation and wrapped it around his body. He immediately felt warmer.

Ivan sensed that he was destroying something between them forever, that it was wrong to treat a woman like that, but he was angry with her now. She appeared to have deceived him in some way and acted too stubbornly, and Ivan subconsciously wanted to punish her.

However, while swearing in his mind, he felt some twinge of embarrassment in his heart. Strangely enough, the separation proved outrageously awkward, and he tried to drown that awkwardness out with anger.

But the girl was still right about something, he was not being entirely fair. And so he could not work up enough anger.

With the jacket on, he took two steps along the trail and turned towards her.

"So, farewell!"

"*Ciao,*" she said without moving, softly and with complete indifference.

That word immediately made him remember their meeting the day before, the happy radiance in her sparkly eyes that had caught his attention back in the forest, her reckless courage under the Germans' noses, and the looks she had given him along the way, full of adoration and some special significance. Ivan was beginning to feel sick at heart. It was neither pity nor sympathy—something was gnawing at his conscience, even though he had nothing to reproach himself for and he did not owe her anything. *No, no*, he said to himself, stifling that feeling. *This is the best thing to do.* He had known from the very beginning that it would be more convenient to go alone. He should have stayed away from her. Now he had clogs on his feet, a jacket over his shoulders and a little bread—it would last longer if he was alone, he would be saving it, limiting his ration to a hundred grammes a day. Alone he would endure anything and get over the ridge. He could not fail, he would get to Trieste, to the partisans even if he had to walk in waist-deep snow. Why had he hooked up with this girl? Who was she to him?

He hurriedly ran to the top of the steep slope, as if fleeing from thoughts about her, abandoned at the bottom, but he was still unable to overcome his frustration. Something deep in his heart was following a different logic. His feet soon slowed down, he took one look over his shoulder, then another—she was still sitting on the slope, a barely visible speck, and all his earlier plans suddenly crumbled at the sight of her resigned helplessness in the face of certain death. In spite of himself, Ivan turned around and ran downhill, his clogs clanging on the trail.

Giulia's body shuddered, and her head shot up in fear when she heard the noise.

"Ivan?"

"Yes."

She grew alert, apparently suspecting something bad.

"Why?"

Without a reply, he threw off the jacket.

"Here. Put it on."

Still sitting on the stone, she quickly wrapped the jacket around herself. He held the sleeves for her and tugged the girl's elbow when she was finished.

"Come here."

Giulia shrank back stubbornly, pulled her elbow free and froze, seemingly afraid of his hands. She looked sternly at his face from under her brow.

"Come here."

"*Non.*"

"Come on, save your *nons.*"

He put his arms around her trembling slender body and lifted it over his shoulder with one heave. She jerked, flopped like a fish, thrashed in his arms, began to babble something, but he ignored her as he flung her behind his back and scooped her up under her knees. She suddenly stopped fighting, dropped silent, hurriedly hooked her hands around his neck, and he felt her warm breath on his cheek and a scalding drop that trickled behind his collar.

"There, there. We'll make it, somehow."

She grew still, pressed herself against his broad back and held her breath. He was breathless too, but that had nothing to do with the wind. Something unfamiliar, imperious and pleasant, big and surprisingly helpless overwhelmed him. Now his recent intention to abandon her actually frightened him, and he rushed uphill, making a racket with his clogs.

13.

By now the snow was thick on the bare stony ground. The clogs were slipping on the trail. Where the climb got steep, Ivan tried to walk sideways, like a skier, to keep his footing under his burden. At first he did not feel the weight of her small body, working his way uphill with strange enthusiasm, supporting her knees a little and hunching his back. Unfortunately, he soon felt the need to stop, straighten up, and draw his breath—his lungs were badly short of air. But he had definitely warmed up. The unrestrained brutality of the high-altitude wind was nothing for his burning skin. Everything inside of him was also on fire, the acid produced by his exhausted body was tearing his lungs apart.

They had to be nearing the pass, for the terrain was gradually flattening out. The trail no longer twisted as it ran over the bare rocky area, covered with a deep layer of snow. A mottled mass that resembled the grey bulk of that lower peak loomed on the right. They must have reached the saddle. By now, the ferocity of the wind had turned into a frenzy. Everything around them roared, groaned and rang, like a gigantic invisible funnel, although the ringing sounds might have been nothing but ear noise. The freezing temperature seemed to have dropped even lower, their hands and knees being especially vulnerable to the cold.

Still, they were lucky that the snow pellets were not wet and did not stick to their clothes. The wind lashed painfully at their faces and rushed on at tremendous speeds. The mountains were roaring and groaning.

They needed rest, but Ivan felt that he was unlikely to get up again if he fell into the snow. And so he dragged Giulia on his back for an hour or more, climbing the twisty path in small steps. Giulia was clinging to him in silence, her fingers twitched on his chest from time to time—he felt those hands and the rest of her body, the warmth on his back, very well. And amazingly, he was cheerful in spite of his fatigue, their recent quarrel and his anger. If only he had more strength, he was ready to carry her, clinging and submissive, a long, long way.

When his legs were already beginning to fail and Ivan became afraid that he would fall, a black fragment of a rock drifted into view out of the chaotic snowy greyness. He immediately left the trail and headed for the rock, his clogs skidding on the stones. Giulia was saying nothing, pressing her cheek tightly to his neck. When they reached the stone, Ivan turned and leaned the girl against it. Her hands unlocked under his chin, his shoulders lightened, and he suddenly realised how heavy she was after all.

"How are you? Cold?"

"*Non, non.*"

"And your feet?"

"Yes," she said softly. "Foots yes."

She looked strangely subdued for her temperament, as if guilty of something before him. He wanted to calm her with some display of kindness and affection, , but his heart was too dried up and slow to produce that kindness. And so he remained very restrained towards her.

Without turning to look at Giulia, he felt her feet with his hands. They were very stiff, apparently swollen, and very cold, colder than his fingers. She gave a little cry at his touch and yanked her feet back.

"Hey, this won't do. Let me have them."

She probably did not understand his words, and so he helped her into a slightly more comfortable position on the rock and gathered some snow granules into his cupped hands.

"Let's give them a rub."

"*Non, non!*"

"Come on, why '*non*'?" he said in a benign but firm voice, grabbed one of her feet, wedged it between his knees, like a blacksmith shoeing a horse, and started rubbing it with snow.

Giulia started yelping and whimpering and tugged against his grip. Ivan chuckled.

"What's wrong? Does it tickle?"

"Hurt. Hurt."

"Hang on a second. I'll be careful."

Working as gently as possible, he rubbed her child-sized foot until it was a little warm and then started on the other. The girl groaned and moaned at first but eventually went quiet.

"Well, are you warm?" he asked, straightening up.

"Warm, warm. Tank you."

"You're welcome."

She wrapped the bottom part of the jacket around her feet, while he leaned against the cold rock and took a moment to calm his breathing. His motionless body immediately became cold—the wind easily penetrated his thin coat, which did nothing to hold his warmth.

"Want some bread?" he asked, recalling their earlier conversation.

"*Non,*" she answered immediately. "Giulia *non* bread. Ivan *essen Brot.*"

"Really? Then we'll save it. It'll come in handy."

Feeling that he was getting cold, Ivan struggled to his feet and offered his back to the girl.

"Well, get on."

Silently but readily, she put her arms around his neck, pulled closer to him, and he immediately grew warmer.

"Ivan," she said softly over the wind, breathing warmth into his ear. "*Du wunderschön*.*"

"Nothing *wunderschön* about me."

She must have grown a little more comfortable on his back, for she regained her persistence and kept asking, emboldened by his kindness towards her, "*Russo alles, alles wunderschön?* Yes?"

"Yes, yes," he would reply, not used to talking about himself. He also wanted to get to the pass as quickly as possible, suspecting that the trail was about to level out, with only meters left to climb.

"True Ivan want scare Giulia? Non? Ivan non leave?"

He smiled uneasily in the darkness and said with a confidence he could believe himself, "Of course not."

"Heavy, yes?"

"No, not at all! Like a feather."

"*Was ist* feter?"

"Well, fluff. A small, small feather."

"Little, little?"

"Yes."

He was walking along the trail, which was clearly visible against the snow-dusted greyness. Her warm breath felt

---

* *Wunderschön* – wonderful (German)

indescribably sweet on the back of his neck. Her flexible thin fingers suddenly stroked his chest, and her unexpected tenderness made him shiver.

"You teach me your tongue *sprechen?*"

"Belarusian?"

"*Ja.*"

He chuckled at her question, so extravagant it seemed under the circumstances.

"Of course," he answered jokingly. "Just let's get to Trieste. Then we'll start."

That humorous thought suddenly whipped up a whole swarm of strange joyous sensations within him. Would they really be so lucky as to reach Trieste and the partisans? If that happened they would not separate, they would join the same unit, she would become his very own. Oh, how much it means to have a kindred spirit at your side in a strange land! Only now did he begin to feel her affectionate attachment to him, and it did not seem unwanted or unnecessary. He felt how desperate he had become during the war in his loneliness—soldiers' camaraderie was still in a different category of relationships. Something sisterly, even motherly had been born between them, and neither words nor actions were necessary. The feeling of intimate harmony was enough to fill him with happiness.

They entered the saddle. The slopes of the peaks were already looming on either side, the trail took them a little higher and then began to descend. Small snowflakes were falling here and there, flitting in the grey darkness.

"Pass?" Giulia stirred on his back.

"Pass, yes."

"Oh, Madonna!"

"Yeah, and you were saying '*kaputt.*' See, we've made it."

He stopped, bent over to pull her higher, but she scrambled to get off his back.

"Giulia herself. *Grazie, danke,* tank you."

"Where will you go barefoot? Stay put."

"*Non* sit. Ivan tired."

"Never mind. It's easy to go down."

He did not let go of her legs, and so she hooked her hands again around his neck, pressed her cheek closer to his unshaven rough jaw and touched her fingers to his equally rough chin.

"Oh, *riccio!* Hedgehog. Prickly."

"We'll shave in Trieste."

"Trieste. Trieste. *Partigiano* Trieste. Ivan, Giulia, *tedescos* ra-ta-ta-ta! *Fascista* scum!" she kept saying, while he was listening with a faint smile and carefully picking his way down the slope.

However, going down was almost as difficult as going up. The clogs slipped frequently, and his knees soon began to ache from constant strain. But the pressure on his chest had eased. His legs were carrying him on their own, and he was working quite hard to slow his pace. Finally, Ivan decided not to restrain himself. He was descending quickly, alternating between fast walking and jogging, stopping occasionally. From time to time, Giulia even got frightened.

"Aah, aah, Ivan!"

"It's nothing. Hold on."

"Aah! Aah!!"

For some reason the wind had eased off, the noise above and around them no longer seemed so loud. That was probably why they felt warmer. Still, it was impossible to tell where the trail led and what lay ahead.

The wind became even weaker after a while, the snow flakes had stopped flitting, mottled patterns broke out on the snow-dusted ground, reaching as far as the eye could see. The trail veered right and left sharply, but the slope was much gentler than the one they had ascended. By now, Ivan was walking at a measured brisk pace and simply trying to stay on the trail in spite of his weariness. Giulia had gone surprisingly quiet. He tried to talk to her, but she did not reply, and he realised that she was asleep.

Having drifted off into slumber on his back, she was breathing evenly under his ear. Her delicate, sensitive hands were lying on his shoulders. The jacket had probably flapped open, and he felt the soft warmth of her small breasts with his back. As if to spite him, a pebble got trapped in one of his clogs. Without reaching down, Ivan was twisting and turning his foot to get it out of the way or shake it out, but the pebble was stubbornly reluctant to move. The struggle became almost torturous, and yet he would not wake her up. Instead, he slowed down and walked at a gentler pace for a very, very long time. He must have also dozed off on his feet, for he suddenly lost track of where they were and who was on his back. However, the lapse lasted only a brief moment. He immediately heard her sigh and relaxed. Everything around them was grey with patches of melting snow on the ground. He felt a puff of damp air drifting from below. The resinous aroma of coniferous forests occasionally hit his nostrils. A waterfall was rumbling not far away, the sound probably coming from a ravine.

At dawn he unexpectedly found himself in the meadow zone.

In an unnoticeable change of scenery, the snowy patches on the ground disappeared. The wind died down, the air grew warmer but also moister. Gloomy wisps of fog were slowly crawling over stones around them. Farther down the slope Ivan became aware of the smell of grass, of flowers and the damp mustiness of the forest, and he knew that the most difficult part was over. He had already lost the trail, but the walking was easy, and he was not looking for it. After taking some more steps, Ivan felt the texture of succulent grass under his feet and thought that he was going to fall. Knee-high stems were slapping his shins with the tight buds of closed flowers. Giulia was still asleep. Quietly so as not to wake the girl, he knelt and carefully lowered himself on his side next to her.

She did not wake up.

14.

For once he did not have his usual painful dream. For several hours his sleep was deep and uninterrupted, then a sticky mixture of fantasy and reality began to whirl and spin in his muddled mind.

At twenty-five youth is flying away, many of the simple human joys cannot be recaptured or experienced if they were not tasted at a younger age. In this respect people probably deserve a slightly better hand than the one dealt to Ivan Tsyareshka by fate. Of course Ivan rarely reflected on this—at home he had to think about finding some way to survive, feed his family, and get a start in life as early as possible. Later, during the war, a far greater burden occupied his mind. He had not loved yet or known a woman. Even so, like many other young people, he was already skeptical about certain relationships between young men and women.

Perhaps he was not to blame after all. The example of acquaintances or relatives sometimes makes up for a lack of personal experience. As it happened, a very colorful episode in Ivan's life made him an unbeliever and a skeptic for a long time.

While serving on the Northwestern Front about two years earlier, he was wounded at the same time as his company commander, Senior Lieutenant Hlebau, who had employed him as an orderly for half a year.

They were attacked while Hlebau was walking through a forest to attend a meeting with the regimental commander. With a gash on his own shoulder, Tsyareshka dragged Hlebau out from under fire, bandaged him up, carried him through the snow over to a road where they were picked up by wagon train drivers. Ivan felt reasonably well with his minor injury, but the company commander's condition was far worse. The senior lieutenant was as white as a sheet and saying almost nothing, only asking to be sent directly to the hospital, bypassing the division's medical unit. The orderly understood the commander's concern—Hlebau did not want to frighten Anyutka, a thin girl with wide open eyes, a nurse in the medical battalion who had until recently been their company's sanitary instructor. Everybody knew that she and Hlebau were most genuinely in love, not just playing the dating game—that was why the company commander had got her transferred to the medical battalion. One way or another, it was a quieter place than the front line. The company's assault riflemen also loved the girl in their own way—respecting the commander, they had to respect his love as well. As for orderly Tsyareshka, he became deeply attached to the girl because he was closer to the unit commander than the others.

As it happened, the medical battalion could not be avoided. How on Earth could Ivan take the wounded man to the hospital if he was afraid that they would not even reach the medical battalion on time? The horses were running swiftly over the well-travelled sled road, and Ivan kept shouting to the driver—a sluggish old soldier wearing two cotton-padded jackets under his greatcoat—to drive the horses harder. Hlebau was becoming incoherent, delirious, loud, he no longer recognised the orderly. Nor did he recognise Anyutka who fell upon the sled with screams when they finally approached the huge canvas tent of the medical battalion.

That evening was sheer agony. Ivan would always remember every detail of it—the starry frozen sky, the gloomy fir trees, the persistent smell of smoke, the quiet voices of people in the ward, and above all, the great inconsolable grief of Anyutka. She was not allowed into the operating room. Even so, with a sheepskin coat draped over her shoulders, she kept trying to get in there and stopped nurses as they left the small ward. Ivan was sitting on a tree stump near the entrance and also hanging on every word about the commander's condition, oblivious to his own pain. But the news was bad—the senior lieutenant's surgery had been long and difficult, a blood transfusion had been performed, and there was a scramble to find some saline solution for him. Anxiety, confusion and tension were in the air, the medics were working hard—both for Anyutka's sake and because the divisional commanders knew Hlebau and valued him. Ivan waited for a long time. He did not try to comfort Anyutka. Feeling awful himself, he just kept smoking until the cigarette case was empty.

Hlebau died during surgery before sutures could be applied.

The sudden tragedy crushed something to dust in Ivan's heart. Indeed, he was surprised himself how personally he had taken the loss—he thought that he had become psychologically accustomed to death during the war. His sufferings must have been increased by another person's grief. Anyutka went off duty for several days and did not visit the wounded, but no one judged her. On the contrary, the young men in stretcher beds in the huge barnlike tent spoke respectfully of such female attachment. Ivan simply kept silent. It was probably at that point that he developed a special attitude towards her. No, it was definitely not love. Rather, he felt something like gratitude to the girl for keeping the memory of the company commander fresh.

Over the long winter evenings in the medical battalion he almost forgot how to joke and smile and just kept smoking cheap, home-produced tobacco and watching the fiery flickering of a brazier fashioned from an iron barrel and heated to a red glow by a paramedic named Akhmetshin. He and Anyutka hardly talked to each other after that evening, well aware of the other's emotional state even without words. Back on duty after her recent break, she lost all of her usual liveliness and grew thoughtful and strict beyond her years. The shared grief bound them together with a quiet reticence. Ivan gave her a hand now and then when she was on duty. His mates understood everything, and none of them wagged their tongues about that girl in his presence.

When his wound healed a little, he fastened his arm to his chest and started taking walks. Together with Akhmetshin, he would wander to a ruined village at the edge of a forest, to a huge German cemetery abandoned by retreating Nazis the previous year. Hundreds and maybe even thousands of crosses were arranged on the ten or so hectares of land in rows that looked as flawless as parade formations from any angle. The lads would chop down those crosses and drag them over to the tents. They were made of dry birch wood with the bark still on them and burnt well. Burning the crosses in the furnace became Ivan's favourite pastime— it was so incredibly soothing to watch fire painstakingly destroy that last reminder of the black scum that had met such an inglorious end in the Russian land. Late at night, after getting her work done, Anyutka would normally sit on his stretcher and also look at the fire. Someone in a dark corner would tell a dreadful tale about the war or a happy story about the time before it. And they would feel good.

However, time passed, patients in the medical battalion came and went. Some patients were evacuated farther back, while others were sent to the front line after they had recovered from their injuries, and one day a seemingly minor change put an instant end to the peaceful serenity of that tent.

Ivan was beginning to collect dirty pots and pans after lunch to take them to the kitchen when he heard voices and footfalls near the tent's entrance and saw two paramedics drag in a stretcher with a wounded man. Lying on the stretcher under a sheepskin coat was a youthful commander with two bars on his black epaulettes. As it later turned out, he belonged to a tank unit that supported their division. Work began to get the major settled in a corner, the battalion political officer himself was giving orders. Ivan briefly wondered why so much attention was being paid to the new arrival, and then just left with the dishes. When he returned shortly, the major was already sitting on the stretcher. He was hot and had thrown off his sheepskin coat, exposing half a dozen medals that glittered proudly on his broad chest. The lads in the ward hushed and turned their heads towards him with interest.

Slightly wounded in both legs, the major turned out to have a glib tongue. Instead of staring vacantly at the wet ceiling like the others, he spent most of his time talking to his neighbours. He quickly made acquaintance with the soldiers and paramedics, and immediately started treating the nurses with the simplicity and vivacity of a friend. In a day or two, fellow officers of the unit became his frequent guests. Commanders stopped by from time to time. Despite the obvious fact that his wounds were not serious, the major soon asked the staff to curtain him off with a sheet. The lads were not surprised—after all, he was a major, and his wish to be somehow distinct from the soldiers was understandable, although unusual in a ward for the lightly wounded. The major's request was honoured, and a cubicle separated with old sheets appeared in the corner. It was there that the most interesting events in the tent unfolded from then on.

Ivan began to frown and barely managed to suppress his seemingly unfounded anger, noticing how much livelier and merrier Anyutka had become and how she never failed to make one more visit to that cubicle on some business or other. The major also noticed the vivacious nurse and started showing her special favour with various gestures. One evening she stayed in the cubicle longer than usual. The major was talking to her about music, about some opera. Anyutka was listening, asking him to repeat, and generally showing excessive interest in his story. She was even late reporting to the duty officer and received a reprimand over the telephone.

After that evening Anyutka became her old self in every way—running up and down the aisle between the stretchers, joking with soldiers and even singing that popular song "The Little Blue Kerchief" on one occasion. She would probably never have seen the perfidious nature of her ways if it had not been for an accidental glance at Ivan. The look he gave her in return must have cut her to the quick, for she stuttered, dropped a bandage roll and ran out of the tent without picking it up. Of course, he said nothing to her, and just thought all the time that it could not be true, she could not be like that, he was wrong, he was imagining things. Another person's love was a constant nagging pain in his heart, and Ivan guarded it as best he could and suffered for it in a way he would probably not have been able to suffer for his own love, a feeling he had never yet experienced.

However, Ivan must have been mistaken trying to calm himself. He soon noticed that Anyutka did not even want to look him in the eye and was constantly itching to get behind the sheets surrounding the cubicle.

A few more days passed like that.

One morning Anyutka was giving the major an injection. The daylight was still faint, and Katyusha rockets were flashing on the other side of the curtains. Alert to any movement in the cubicle, Ivan was sweeping the earth aisle in the tent with a broom of fir tree branches when he suddenly saw very eloquent shadows on the sheets.

He saw Anyutka jerk in fear against the major's tenacious grip, but then she froze and stifled a cry. Ivan shuddered involuntarily, as if shot through with electricity, then cursed with unexpected anger, threw the broom underfoot and plopped face down on his threadbare bed.

He lay for a long time without hearing what was happening in the tent or getting up for breakfast, and when the morning fuss subsided, he gathered his clothes, tied his knapsack shut and left without any goodbyes.

By noon he had already rejoined his company.

The sergeant major who visited the medical battalion a day later to collect his ration certificate, brought back an unseemly piece of gossip about Tsyareshka's weird stunt. His mates teased him for a while and then calmed down, while Ivan simply kept smoking in silence, certain that no one would understand what was going on in his heart.

15.

His first sensation in the real world was one of warmth.

The air was actually not warm but hot, stuffy, misty. In his drowsy state he saw himself lying on a stretcher near the brazier, which had been mercilessly stoked by Akhmetshin. However, the heat was affecting his head and shoulders even more than his feet. Ivan felt the sticky wetness of sweat and was longing to turn over and somehow shield himself from that debilitating heat but found himself unable to even open his eyes, so strong was the grip of his sleepy fatigue.

He suffered in his slumber like that for a long time, until sleep began to retreat and his mind slowly started to wake up and take over his tired body. He stirred, stretched, put out his hand, and sensed the dewy coldness of grass with his palm. Surprised, he willed himself to open his eyes, and the first thing he saw was a bright red flower next to his face.

Tilted towards the light, it was affectionately offering its four glossy petals to the sun. A red drop as pure as a tear was sparkling on the edge of one of the petals, ready to fall at any moment. A light wind that felt like a morning breeze was gently stirring the flower's long, thin stem. A bumble bee buzzed among the thick bright mix of grasses for a long time and then suddenly disappeared. Its deep bass voice abruptly broke off, and it dawned on Ivan that the world around him had fallen completely silent. He had already forgotten what silence was like and found it frightening.

Not knowing where he was, Ivan jerked, sat up, opening his sleepy sore eyes wide, looked around, and gasped at the extraordinary, almost fairytale beauty of the landscape around him.

The whole surface of the vast sunny slope looked like a lake shining with the bright crimsons of Alpine poppy flowers.

Tall, broad-leaved, apparently untrampled by human feet and nurtured by the great generosity of nature, millions of flowers were rippling a solemn red and stirring gently in the light wind throughout that mountain-framed meadow, stretching all the way to a dark green stand of coniferous trees far below. Ivan, however, immediately turned sullen when he looked farther into the distance. Far beyond the valley, the same towering bear's ridge continued to stand out against the sky with blue streaks of snow. It was clearly much taller than the ridge they had crossed, the twin summits protruding behind their backs, for although the sun was already high in the sky, the clear blueish haze of its shadow covered half of the narrow valley. With nothing screening it from view now, the ridge remained a distant and inaccessible glittering giant, looking probably the same as the previous day.

All of a sudden, Ivan started in alarm—only now did his mind grasp the disturbing significance of silence. A shiver ran up his spine—where was Giulia? He spun on the ground again, looked around but saw no one. Her solitary leather jacket lay nearby, spread out on her resting place of flattened poppies. Ivan slapped himself on the chest—there was nothing beneath his coat, its bottom was carelessly untucked. However, his initial anxiety immediately subsided—the pistol and the ragged one-third of the loaf lay in the grass under the jacket's sleeve, apparently hidden from the sun. Ivan jumped to his feet and frantically started scanning the bottom of the slope. A bleak sadness surged into his heart—where was she? An ugly suspicion began to take shape in his mind, but he could not believe it. Why not, he probably did not know, he only wanted to see, hear and feel her nearby. He suddenly found his loneliness more upsetting than any failure.

Ivan grabbed the pistol and the bread, scooped the jacket under his arm, and leapt into the grass. The tall dewy flowers tickled his swollen, scratched and bruised feet. He thought about the clogs and looked at the ground, but they were not there. Anxiety seized him again—could that be true? He quickly walked barefoot across the meadow, slapping his legs against cluster upon cluster of poppy plants. Ivan had gone far down the slope when he suddenly stopped and looked back—his trail was visible in the dense tangle of flowers. A sea of red untouched by any living creature surrounded him.

An idea formed in his mind. Ivan adjusted the garment under his arm and quickly headed back to their resting place.

Another track was indeed visible in the grass—from his vantage point, he could see that it ran at an angle to the mouth of a gully, and he hurried along the faint trail left by Giulia. His feet and trouser legs soon became wet with dew. All around him were poppy flowers, magical in their sunny beauty. His head was swimming from the strong fragrant aroma. As always, he was very hungry, and his vision was a little blurry from fatigue and weakness. However, he was accustomed to such sensations. Naturally strong and seasoned by hardship, his body was coping tolerably well, and Ivan felt that he still had some energy left.

With a heavy heart he ran around thorny rhododendron shrubs that were studded with fist-sized red flowers. From the small gully ahead of him came the noise of a waterfall. He soon reached a grassy swell, and the noise drew extremely close. A glittering stream was pouring out of the waterfall's glistening stone lip and breaking against a rock. Tiny droplets of spray were whirling in the misty haze around it, and a small multicoloured patch of real rainbow was hanging in the air against the gloomy background of stone. Oblivious to that unexpected generosity of the mountains, Ivan kept climbing until he suddenly gasped, stopped, hunched to the ground, and froze. Giulia was standing on a stone a hundred or so steps away with her back towards him and bathing under the showery sprinkle of falling water, with only her arms covering her.

He recognised her at once, although she was wearing absolutely nothing. Naked, she immediately lost the hateful marks of a *Häftling* and changed beyond recognition in her timid female modesty, full of mystery and beauty, as she found herself alone with nature. Of course, the girl had not seen him. She was patiently keeping her skinny, light body under the thick veil of splashing, streaming water, wary, tense and seemingly ready to shrink and disappear at the slightest noise. The colourful reflection of the rainbow was playing over her sharp shoulders as they sparkled with spray.

Unable to overcome an embarrassed and joyful feeling, Ivan slowly lowered himself to the grass, lay on his back, rolled over, and the crystal-clear cloudless sky also rolled over above him. The damp mustiness of the earth went to his head like an intoxicating brew and made him dizzy.

He sprawled on the cool grassy turf and laughed under his breath in anticipation of something uncertain but joyful.

An inextinguishable fire of anxiety was still smouldering in the recesses of his consciousness—an apparently unassailable ridge lay ahead of them. Behind their backs...Well, it was clear what could come along their tracks from the camp. However, in that sanctuary of beauty, after losing and finding a dear person, Ivan began to feel a kind of childlike joy and happiness that he had probably never felt in his short life. And he was thirstily drinking that unexpected happiness with all his heart, not even trying to figure out where it came from and what had happened to him. He was simply experiencing human happiness, that was all. Of course, he soon realised that the experience would be short-lived. Something worrisome and dark would not let go of him even in that moment of happiness, something was troubling and weighing him down, but Ivan suppressed and stifled it because he felt so indescribably good.

He was no longer peeking out of the poppies and did not give her a single look. Shy tactfulness prevented him from doing that, however strong the temptation was. Lying flat on his stomach, he was plucking out poppy plants and absent-mindedly arranging their branchy flowers into a bouquet.

Full of inexpressible joy, Ivan was busy gathering flowers when he heard hasty footsteps a short distance away and popped his head above the grass. There was nobody under the waterfall. Putting on her striped coat, Giulia was running down the slope and seemed to be looking for the place where she had left him. He gave another soft chuckle when he saw her impatient and anxious distant gaze. However, instead of calling out to her, he gathered the jacket and slowly started after her.

With her wet jet-black hair glistening in the sun, she quickly ran around the rhododendron and stumbled to a halt near their resting place. Even from a distance, he could see her fear and confusion. A second later, she looked one way, then another, then headed downhill, and then looked back and stopped.

"Ivan!!!"

Fear, pain and joy came together in that call. She clapped her hands and darted towards him like a bird. Ivan stopped. An eternity seemed to have passed since he had last seen those joyous, sparkly eyes, those delicate features of her swarthy face, that disorderly scattering of her close-cropped hair. Everything inside him strained towards her, but he suppressed his urge and held himself back, God knows why. Not so Giulia, who ran over to him, trampling the poppy with her clogs, threw her arms around him, hung on his neck and planted a kiss near his lips, drunken and sudden as a gunshot.

"*Ivanio!!!*"

He simply held his breath, while Giulia, still holding on to his neck, leaned back impetuously and gave a happy and carefree laugh, peering with affection at his face, which was still burning from the cold fire of her lips. Continuing to laugh, she released her fingers, pushed him lightly and sat on the grass opposite him, resting on her outstretched arms. Her eyes were gleaming with effervescent, mischievously playful laughter, her coat, carelessly closed with only one stick-shaped button, flapped open, and a small blue enamel cross flashed in the wedge-like depression between her breasts. The cross drew his attention like a needle prick.

She caught his gaze and made a slightly belated adjustment, covering herself and continuing to laugh with her eyes, face and big, white-toothed mouth—every fibre of her young being cool and fresh after bathing.

But Ivan had changed beyond recognition. He grew sullen and flustered, sensing after half a minute of standing next to her that something inside of him was breaking down, something was waning, some unknown new force was subduing his will. At the same time, he began to feel, rather vaguely at first, that he should resist, hold his own, not yield. Indeed, her bold, thoughtless pounce rattled him and made him wonder, *Why should she act like that? How is it possible? Why? Was it joy, impulse? Or maybe?..*

Despite his sullenness and embarrassment, he took a step closer to her. Giulia's laughter suddenly broke off, and she launched herself towards him.

"Ivan!" she clapped her hands together, spotting the flowers in his hands. "*Ist* dis surprise *signorina*? Yes? Yes?"

The bunch of poppy flowers in his hands came as a surprise even to Ivan as he looked at them in bewilderment and burst out laughing. She also began to laugh and smelled the flowers, burying her elegant face in the bouquet. Then she put the bouquet down on the grass and hurriedly started plucking out poppy flowers around her.

"Giulia tanks Ivan. Tank very, very."

"Oh, no, stop it," he faltered.

"Tank very, very necessary. Ivan save signorina. *Russo* save *Italiano. Das ist internazionale. Fraternità*," she was saying, half jokingly, as she pulled out more and more flowers. Then she ran over to Ivan and dumped an armful of them upon his chest.

"Oh, please," he said in bewilderment. "It makes no sense!"

"Necessary! Necessary," she kept saying in Russian with a funny accent, and he was forced to accept not only the flowers but also the jacket with the bread wrapped in it. She must have felt the shape of the loaf in the jacket with her hands, for she grew more serious.

"*Brot?*"

"Yes, let's eat," Ivan perked up, recovering from his embarrassment, put everything on the ground, and sat down himself.

She quickly sat beside him.

16.

"Wish we could eat it all now," Ivan said, holding a kilogramme or so of dry bread with crumbling edges, hard, but still so appetizing and desirable that both were looking at it and drooling almost uncontrollably.

"All, all," Giulia echoed eagerly, her eyes also glued to the loaf.

After a brief hesitation, Ivan looked over her head at the distant snowy ridge. "No, we can't," he sighed.

"Can't? *Non?*"

"No."

She understood him and also sighed, while Ivan spread the jacket on the ground and placed their meagre ration on the leather. He now had an important job to do—deal out two equal portions and make as few crumbs as possible. Without a knife, they had nothing to cut the bread with.

And so he carefully broke the bread, arranging small pieces into two piles, ever conscious of Giulia's inability to control her hunger. A new feeling was welling up within his heart, something brotherly or maybe fatherly. Noble and powerful, it was filling him with goodwill towards her, so childishly unaccustomed to the great adversities of war and so thoughtlessly resolute in her almost subconscious, bird-like hunger for freedom.

Ivan was busily dividing the bread. Every piece of crust, every crumb was weighed by their watchful eyes, and he intentionally made one pile bigger by putting more crusts into it. Together with the ends of a loaf, scraps of crust were much more valuable by camp standards than tiny bits and pieces without crust of the same weight. When everything had been divided, Ivan stuffed the two hundred grammes or so of leftovers into a jacket pocket.

"That one is for you, and this is for me," he said simply, without the traditional ritual of negotiations, and pushed the pile with an end slice towards her.

Her jet-black brows shot up.

"No. Dis is Ivan, dis is Giulia," she swapped the piles.

He looked her in the eye and smiled kind-heartedly.

"No, Giulia, please. This is for you."

Ivan hastily took his portion. Giulia gave him a suspicious look, wrinkled her face and then deftly shoved one crust into his hands. He immediately started towards her, but she chuckled and hurriedly drew away, throwing up her hands to keep her portion out of his reach. Ivan pressed with playful stubbornness, but she twisted out of the way, touched his side with her bosom and clutched at his shoulder to keep her footing. Her laughter ceased abruptly. He felt a strange tingle of embarrassment at that unexpected closeness. Suppressing a new, yet unconscious desire, he immediately drew back from her and sat on the edge of the jacket, while she bit her lip and adjusted the front of her coat, peeking at him from under her brow with a mischievous, girlish smile.

"Take it and eat. It's yours, you know," he said, sliding the crust over the bottom of the jacket.

"*Non.*"

She started gnawing her bread end with a good-natured lightness of spirit, flashing her perfectly white teeth.

"Take it, I say."

"*Non.*"

"Take it."

"*Non,*" she persisted, laughing with her eyes.

"You won't give way, will you? Okay, do as you wish," Ivan said and took a bite of his portion.

She was soon done with hers. Predictably far from satisfied, she was stealing looks at the bulging pocket of the jacket. Ivan was chewing slowly, drawing out the pleasure, noticing all her looks, and gradually beginning to wonder whether he should eat it all. Those grammes would not make much of a meal the next time, but now they would definitely hit the spot. However, he chased those thoughts away by an effort of will, knowing too well the value of even such a tiny portion.

"Want more?" he asked, finally finishing his meal.

Giulia shook her head an emphatic "No", as if fearing that she would change her mind, "*Non! Non!*"

"And this?" he nodded at the crust that still lay in the middle of the jacket.

"Giulia *non.*"

"Okay, let's divide it in half then."

"*Was ist das*—half?"

The girl wrinkled up her nose inquiringly. The sun was shining in her face, and she was constantly making grimaces, as if to tease him.

"Well, a little to Ivan, a little to Giulia."

He broke the crust apart and gave her one half—she hesitantly took it, bit off a small piece, and chewed it.

"*Gut. Häftlingen cioccolato.*"

"That's what the Germans do to you. Even bread tastes like chocolate."

"Giulia run *Napoli,* eat *cioccolato. Brot* was little, *cioccolato* much," she said, still squinting her coal-black eyes.

"You were fleeing to *Napoli?*"

"Si. *Roma* run. *Vater* run."

"From your father? Why?"

"Ah, *una.* One *storia,*" she replied reluctantly, bit off another small piece and chewed it. Then she pored over the crust. "*Vater* want bad *marito.* Russian *ist* husband."

Husband! She was married! the news struck him as unexpectedly bleak as it hit home, and the girl suddenly became unpleasant and undesirable. Giulia probably sensed that, for she glanced at his face out of the corner of her lively eyes and smiled.

"*Non marito. Signore* Giangarini *non* husband was. Giulia *non* want *signore* Giangarini."

Still in low spirits, Ivan asked, "And why didn't you want him?"

"Oh, it was *un segreto.*"

"What secret?"

Casting mischievous looks right, left and sideways at him, the twinkle-eyed Giulia was sucking on her crust, while he was sitting with his eyes on the ground and ripping out clumps of grass roots and all.

"Oh, *segreto!* Little *segreto.* Giulia love, love. How it in Russian? *Uno giovanotto** Mario. Fellow Mario."

"Oh, did you?" he said and tossed the grass aside. The wind immediately scattered the blades in the air.

Ivan turned away. For some reason, he no longer wanted to look at her and just listened grimly.

---

*   *Giovanotto* – young man (Italian)

But Giulia carried on, seemingly oblivious to his mood change, "*Gut* fellow was. Giulia take *pistole,* run Mario *Napoli. Napoli guerra,* war. *Italiano schiessen Deutsch.* Giulia *schiessen.*" She sighed. "*Partigiano Italiano* little, *Deutsch* many. Many *Italiano* kill. Many camp. Giulia camp. Very bad camp!"

"Why, did you two fight Germans?" Ivan asked with cheerless curiosity, foreseeing the answer.

"*Si.* Yes."

"Wow!" he said in a surprised but restrained voice and asked, "And where is your Mario?"

She did not reply at once. Pulling her knees to her chest, she hooked her hands around her long shins, put her chin on them and looked into the distance.

"Mario *fu ucciso.*"

"Killed?"

"Yes."

Both kept silent for a while. For some reason, Ivan immediately felt relief, as if leaving behind something unpleasant. He gave her a look—she met it with seriousness, but then her eyes quickly began to lose their underlying tinge of sadness and grow warmer under his gaze. Her short-lived sadness melted away and she started to laugh.

"Why Ivan look so?"

"Never mind."

"*Was ist* mind?"

"Mind is mind. Let's go to Trieste."

"Oh, Trieste!" she jumped up lightly from the grass.

He also got up and swung the jacket over his shoulder with an unexpected lightness of spirit. Together they made their way down the poppy meadow.

The sun was getting hotter and hotter. The shadow of the bear's ridge in the valley was gradually narrowing, sultry ashen mist was rippling at the foot of a distant mountain and enveloping the woody slopes. Only the snowy ridges overhead were shining confidently, showing off every faded patch on their mottled sides.

"Trieste *gut!* Trieste *partigiano!* Trieste sea!" Giulia was saying in an animated voice. In an apparent rush of inspiration, she began to sing,

"*Mi par d'udire ancora,*

La voce tua, in mezzo ai fior.*"

Playfully making eyes at him, she was shaping unfamiliar words quietly but very rhythmically, and their strangeness made them even more melodic. He did not know the song. Its tuneful melody swirled and hovered in the air, something about its rhythm resembled the gentle roll of the sea, something affectionate and good was issuing steadily from his heart.

"*Per non sofrire,*

Per non morire

*Io te penso, e ti amo...***"

Ivan listened with bated breath to that euphonious echo of a different, unknown world. All of a sudden the girl's singing ceased, and she started towards him.

"Ivan! Learn Giulia 'Katusha!'"

"'Katyusha?'"

"Sì. 'Katusha.'"

---

*   *Mi par d'udire ancora,/La voce tua, in mezzo ai fior* - It seems to me I still can hear/Your voice among the flowers (Italian)

**   *Per non sofrire,/Per non morire /Io te penso, e ti amo* – So as not to suffer,/not to die/You I think about and love (Italian)

"All in bloom are the apple trees and pear trees

O'er the river the mists come sweeping in," she sang, tossing her head, while he chuckled, so wrong and so childishly lame the lines sounded, although she caught the tune rather well.

Like a diligent schoolgirl, she started singing "Katyusha," getting the words a little mixed up, and he was amused and happy with her, the way an adult feels with a jovial, cute, and obedient child. He was walking close to Giulia and smiling in his heart from a quiet human happiness he had not experienced for such a long time. The cause of that happiness was unclear. Could it be the high clear sky, or the beauty of the mountains, or the limitless expanse that lay before them, or, perhaps, the never-before-seen magical abundance of flowers, or even the marvelous smells mixed into one fragrant aroma? Something festive, movingly cordial was floating over those mountains and the meadow. It was actually difficult to believe in danger, captivity and the possibility of pursuit, and he wondered whether the previous six months of horrors with SS officers, death, the stench of crematories and the non-stop barking of Alsatians had been a dream. And if that was all reality, how could the immortal beauty of nature co-exist with it, what kind of great life power had separated and detached nature's purity from man's criminal madness? Alas, those disgusting things were not a dream or a ghost—the stripes and circles on their clothes reminded them every minute of what had happened and what they had not yet completely escaped. And now, amid the pristine purity of nature, their clothes struck him as such an insult to humanity that Ivan hurriedly stripped off his coat and wrapped the jacket around it to hide it from view. Giulia stopped singing and examined his slightly suntanned, rugged, strong shoulders with a smile.

"Oh, *Ercole*—Hercules! *Russo* Hercules!"

"Oh, yeah, Hercules. A pushover," Ivan said.

"*Non, non!* Hercules!"

She jokingly slapped his bare shoulder blade and clasped his lowered arm.

"Strong, *gut Russo.* Why camp go?"

"Why I went? They brought me there, that's why."

"You must fought *fascisti!*" she swung her small fist in the air.

"I fought as long as I could. But…"

Raising his elbow, he turned his other side to her, and a sympathetic, almost fearful expression immediately appeared on her lively, giggly face.

"Oh, oh! *Santa Maria!*"

"A Hercules all right," he sighed.

"Hurt?" she kept asking and carefully touched the huge wide scar—a mark left by a knife bayonet.

He boldly rubbed his side.

"Not any longer. The hurting's over."

"Oh, oh!"

"Come on, don't be afraid, you odd little thing," he said affectionately. "Now, jab me harder."

Seeing her hesitation, he took her slender fingers in his hand and pressed them against the scar. She gave a little cry of fear and recoiled. Ivan held her shoulders, and the brief touch of her fingers sent an intoxicating rush of excitement into his blood. In spite of himself, Ivan drew back. *No, this is wrong! What am I doing? It's wrong. I should go, I've got to make it and get out of this nest of Nazi vipers—that's why I escaped.*

"Now, listen," he frowned after a quick glance at her. "We should, we should go quickly. Understand?"

"*Ja,*" she agreed, smiling and looking into his eyes with some thought in the back of her mind.

17.

They descended from the top of the meadow to the middle. The poppies began to part, giving way to the invasive profusion of other flowers. Blue patches of tall fragrant forget-me-nots were rippling here and there, bellflowers were swaying in the wind, the rich aroma of yellow azalea was making their heads swim. The flower thickets were interspersed with gravelly spots and grey stones protruding from the grass. Prickly debris lay thick around all stones, injuring their feet. Ivan began to choose his path more carefully, peering at the ground. At one point, a red droplet flashed in the grass in front of him. He bent over. Several large juice-filled strawberries were sparkling among small toothed leaves. No sooner had he picked them than more red blinking stars lit up before his eyes. He put down the jacket and squatted. With a cry of joy Giulia also scrambled to the ground.

There were plenty of berries—large, juicy, and ripe almost without exception. Ivan and Giulia began to crawl around and eat, eat hungrily, from cupped hands, forgetting about time and caution. A lot of time probably passed. The sun moved over to the other side of the sky and was casting bright light over the sparsely wooded valley and the bear's ridge, riven with twisting ravines.

Dripping sweat, Ivan was still crawling around in the grass on his knees when he heard Giulia's footsteps behind him. He looked back, turned and sat down, wiping his forehead. With a kind smile lurking behind her sparkly eyes, the girl hurriedly approached him, knelt down, and opened the folded edge of her coat. Lying on the striped fabric, which was heavily stained with strawberry juice, was a loose pile of red berries.

"*Bitte**, *Russo* Ivan," she ceremoniously offered the fruit to him.

"Oh, please! I've had enough!"

"*Non* enough! *Essen!*"

She scooped some berries with her hand and almost forced him to eat them. Then she ate a little herself and brought her cupped hands back to his mouth. For some reason, the strawberries eaten out of her hands had a completely different taste. He picked them out of the pile with his lips and gave her warm flagrant palm a playful tickle with his teeth.

"*Non, non!*" Giulia threatened mischievously.

Thus they finished her stock of berries, and Ivan collected the jacket from a nearby cluster of poppy plants.

"*Ayda?*"

"*Ayda!*" she agreed boldly.

Feeling satisfied and somehow closer to each other, they resumed their downhill walk. Giulia put a trusting hand on his shoulder.

"Strawberries are good," he said, breaking tthe peaceful and friendly but slightly uneasy silence. "I'd fed on them for many summers before the war."

---

*   *Bitte* – please (German)

"Oh, *Russo, vegetariani?*" she asked in surprise. "Giulia *non vegetariani.* Giulia like beef steak, spaghetti, omelet."

"Macaroni as well," he added, and they both laughed.

"*Sì, sì* macaroni," she confirmed and said a little mockingly, "And *Russo*—storberries!"

"Yes, sometimes. How can you help it? If the harvest is poor, you get hungry," Ivan agreed sadly.

Giulia gave him a surprised look.

"Why hungry? *Russland* how hungry? *Russland* most richest. Truth?"

"True, everything is true."

"Why hunger? Talk!" she persisted, apparently alarmed by his words.

He kept silent for a while, walking on the grass and wondering whether he should tell her about it. However, he had already tasted the benevolent lenience of her heart and now found himself drawn towards it against his will. A long-forgotten need for sincerity awoke within him.

"We starved in 1933, for example, because of drought."

"*Was ist* drought?"

"What's a drought?" He bent over and plucked out a fistful of grass. "It's when the sun burns everything down, including grass. Hunger is what killed my father."

So surprised was Giulia that she stopped, her strict face darkened, and she eyed Ivan with a testing, suspicious look. She said nothing, just let go of his hand and immediately withdrew into herself. Saddened by the bleak memory, he walked on in silence.

Yes, there were difficult years in their parts. They were usually saved by potatoes, but even potatoes sometimes ran out by the new harvest, and grass then appeared on the tables of peasants. They cooked some brew from sorrel and nettle and made grass pancakes, adding a handful of flour. He would remember their rancid taste all his life.

In 1933, when things got particularly bad, Ivan's father left everything and went to Ukraine to look for work and food. Ivan's mother ended up with a bloated stomach, his little siblings were barely walking. They were lucky to have a cow and new potatoes. Father came back towards the autumn. His health had not been very good before, but now it failed completely. He went to bed and never got up until Christmas. He was buried on Christmas Day, survived by four little children. Ivan, the eldest, had to feed and bring them up. Oh, what a difficult time he had! That was the painful truth of his life. But how could you talk about it?

He was walking deep in thought, looking down at her flashing blue-grey clogs and the slowly drifting and stirring shadows of their two short figures. Giulia, however, began to fall behind, and he sensed some change in her mood but did not look back.

"And was Siberia? Was bad kolkoz?" the girl called out from behind with an obvious challenge and a sudden coldness in her eyes.

He stopped and gave her an attentive look.

"Who told you this?"

"One bad *Russo* said. You want to say. I knowed!"

"Me?"

"You! Talk!"

"I don't want anything. What can I tell you?"

"Say *das* Giulia *non* truth. Giulia mistake!'"

Her face grew angry, her eyes were glaring, all her goodwill towards him was gone, and he was straining to understand the cause of that change as well as the meaning of her very unpleasant questions.

"You, talk! Talk!"

She seemed to have indeed heard something, in the camp or, maybe, while she was still in Rome. But he could not confirm her guesses now, he was already sorry to have mentioned the famine.

"Injustice was?" the girl pressed him.

"What injustice? What are you talking about?"

"*Innocente* people to Siberia sent?"

He looked searchingly into her sharp eyes and felt that he had to either tell the truth or invent some lie. However, he did not know how to lie.

"Yes, the kulaks* were," Ivan said brusquely to put a quick end to that frustrating conversation.

Giulia bit her lip in anguish.

"*Non* truth!" she suddenly cried out and gave him a glance that felt like a blow, so much pain, resentment and the most explicit hostility her eyes expressed.

"*Non* truth. *Non*. Ivan is like Vlasov**."

All of a sudden she sniffled loudly and covered her face with her hands. Ivan's heart trembled as he started towards her, but she stopped him with an adamant, infuriated "*Non!*" and ran down the hill. He stood still, not knowing what to do and just looking at her back in confusion. His thoughts suddenly got mixed up, and he felt that something bad had happened but did not know what had gone wrong and how to set things right.

---

*   *Kulak* – wealthy farmer (Belarusian)

**   Andrei Vlasov, Red Army general who went over to the Germans in 1942

Giulia ran over to a gravelly flowerless knoll, sat down, reached forward, and drew up her knees without giving him a single look.

Well, well. Vlasov! Ivan said to himself in bewilderment, sighed and started stamping around in the grass.

He must have done something really wrong. He had undermined her goodwill so inappropriately, despite working so hard to forge that human bond and becoming dependent on it. Everything inside of him began to ache from that thought, his quiet joy immediately faded, and he felt very lonely at heart.

Naturally she had already heard some of what had been going on in his country before the war, perhaps, something far removed from the truth. But how could he explain it to her to make everything clear? Never in his life had he said anything to anyone about those dreadful years—even to his own people, let alone foreigners. That was the best thing to do. After all, his people knew everything as well as he did, and his stories would not surprise anyone. Of course, lads in the camp would sometimes strike up conversations about the past, but in the presence of people from other countries they would only boast about the beauty of their nature and their wellbeing. That made sense—who does not want to look better than he is in reality, whose heart does not bleed for his own homeland? However, Ivan usually said nothing during such conversations. He knew nothing of boasting and simply had no wish to pick over the difficult things that had once happened in his country, not understanding many of them himself yet.

Flipping the jacket from shoulder to shoulder, Ivan was stamping around in the grass. The sun was beating down on the back of his head and his shoulders. However hard he thought, he could not understand what had happened between them and what his fault was. Of course, it would have been better to keep silent about the famine. As for her dark suspicions, he should probably have tried harder to convince the girl of the justice of our life. Although it would be very difficult to explain to her the kind of struggle that had been going on in his land at that time, it was probably necessary to try. After all, it would be so unfortunate to lose her trust and respect. Perhaps it would be no crime to tell a few lies. However, Ivan felt, still vaguely, that it was not about him, there was something absolutely huge standing behind his back and would make any trickery look disgusting.

But now who knew what he should expect? One could imagine Giulia's reaction to his frankness and truth. Could she understand all the complexity of what had once caused him so much anguish?

Come what might! With his few but honestly lived years and all his faith and sincerity, could he possibly lose something in the eyes of that Westerner only because of the hard times in his life? Could beautiful lies wrapped in Western-style packaging possibly be more valuable than the truth, even if it was bitter? No! If that girl had a sensitive heart, she would understand him and do justice to him and his people, who deserved respect. Having understood that with great clarity, Ivan became more comfortable and composed. It was as if something had already been decided and he only had to wait for an outcome.

18.

However, his patience ran out too quickly.

With her back turned towards him, the offended Giulia was sitting aloof and thoughtfully picking at the ground. After some reflection Ivan took the jacket and started walking towards her slowly. She heard his footsteps, shuddered, shot a furious look at him, and then jumped to her feet and beat a retreat. He slowly climbed the knoll and stopped. He had to wait or, maybe, go—he simply did not know what to do. Giulia ran farther down the meadow and, without looking back, hid behind a huge stone, whose massive top protruded over the grass.

He threw the jacket to the ground and lay down upon it on his stomach, determined to wait and see what would happen next.

The air grew hot. Heated by the sun and overgrown with grass that was as coarse as the crust of brown bread rolls, the hard limestone knoll was radiating dry dusty heat like a fiery furnace. Ivan's bare shoulders and back were melting from the sweaty heat. Tiny coloured insects were flitting and fluttering around in the grass. Ivan kept his eyes on the stone that was hiding Giulia from view, but she would not come out. Fatigue, heat, and the uncertainty of waiting were making him drowsy. His hunger abated, probably dulled by the berries or the heat, but he became thirsty. *It never rains but it pours,* Ivan thought. They had to go, reach the snowy ridge as soon as possible, find some pass, get food, and start what Ivan felt would be an exceedingly difficult climb. And yet there he was lying and waiting. Initially rather successful, his attempt to escape had indeed taken a most inappropriate turn. He began to hack at the ground with a bit of stone to ward off sleep. A large black beetle with huge pincers appeared in front of his face from some place in the grass. Apparently surprised by the unexpected encounter, it stopped, popped out its crayfish eyes and waited, menacingly moving its long, flexible antennae. At a mere touch of Ivan's finger the beetle stretched out all its six legs and froze. Ivan put out his hand to flick away that rather unpleasant creature when he suddenly heard footsteps behind his back. He spun on the ground so deftly that his reaction must have caught the human off guard, for the man gave an audible hiccup and simultaneously jumped aside with extraordinary agility. Having come extremely close, he was now warily standing in the grass, staring at Ivan with inhuman eyes. It was the mad German.

"Hello!" Ivan smiled ironically. "Doing fine, huh?"

Ivan was quite surprised. He had certainly not expected to see the madman there, so wild, haunted, black from sweat and dirt, with an almost inhuman expression on his dry face, wearing an unbuttoned coat and tattered trousers. Moreover, the German was limping and putting almost no weight on one foot. And yet, lo and behold, that plodder had made it to the meadow. Given his condition, his persistence was simply enviable—like a ghost, he had tirelessly trudged after them, counting on God knows what.

"*Brot!*" the German said quietly but with a noticeable touch of meek despair in his voice.

"*Brot* again?" Ivan asked spitefully. "Are we your keepers?"

The madman took a few hesitant steps towards Ivan.

"*Brot!*"

"Why, you wanted to go to the Gestapo. To your Hitler."

"*Nichts* Hitler. Hitler *kaputt*."

"*Kaputt?* Now you're talking."

Hardly able to understand him, the madman was waiting patiently and warily with his bony arms spread out.

Ivan slipped his hand into the jacket and broke off a small piece of the crust without taking out the loaf. Noticing it in Ivan's hands, the German brightened, his eyes lit up, his trembling hands in tattered sleeves reached forward.

"*Brot! Brot!*"

"Take it. And get lost."

Ivan flung the bread to him, but the German failed to catch it. He scrambled to the ground, grabbed the crust with both hands together with grass and sand, and jumped back to his feet. Then, casting fearful looks over his shoulder, he worked his way sideways down the slope, apparently expecting a pursuit.

Maybe this will get him out of the way, Ivan thought. They would be safer with the *Häftling* ahead of them and not walking behind all the time. Ivan followed his figure with a thoughtful gaze until it disappeared in the ravine, then he lay down on the jacket again.

The anger he had felt for that man the previous day had vanished, but it had not been replaced with goodwill— the pain of losses and the memory of the people who had perished at the hands of this German's compatriots were still very fresh in his heart. Of course, he could be a convinced antifascist, but what was the use of that conviction if his mind had been completely ruined? However, it seemed more likely that the German was some reject of their beastly system and had simply had bad luck in their inhuman service. Such people could also be found in the concentration camp. To give just one example, their *Kommandoführer* would hardly get a pat on the back for their escape and the bomb explosion, if, indeed, he managed to recover. He could also be thrown behind the wire instead of those who caught him off guard. Even so, he would probably be appointed a *Kapo** and also empowered to destroy, despite being a *Häftling*. And just as he had been a dog, a dog he would remain, except that his personal misfortune might make him even more hateful of the prisoners. He could still cause a lot of misery to people.

The Nazis had achieved a great deal through their *Entmenschung***, the most dastardly of all evil deeds on the Earth. And while one could still make some sense of their animal brutality towards enemies, their ruthlessness towards their own people who had somehow displeased their superiors was simply striking. Fear of punishment became their be all and end all. Everybody lived under the threat of being reprimanded, punished, demoted and sent to the front line, in danger of exposing their families to persecution. And that was probably why, given permission, they committed such atrocities and took revenge on those who were weaker, on prisoners, inmates of concentration camps and Jews. It was surprising that the Germans in the front line were still stubborn fighters. They might have been

---

*   *Kapo* – concentration camp prisoner appointed by the SS to perform certain tasks

**   *Entmenschung* – dehumanisation (German)

that way because their fear of punishment acquired a new dimension under fire—a military tribunal or a Soviet bullet were their only options. Even so, the nature of heroism is very complex, and Ivan did not like to reflect upon it, especially since he did not consider himself heroic or even brave. Had he been a hero, he would not have allowed himself to be captured and would have done something at that most decisive moment, which seemed to have determined both his future and his past forever. He should probably have killed himself, and that would have been the end of it. In a fleeting moment he recalled that day and the knife-shaped bayonet, sooty from firing, which he glimpsed when he rolled out from under the tank. The bayonet and the boot with a canvas strap in its broad shaft and the long handle of the grenade.

The stubbled German, covered with a ghastly layer of dust, was shouting something, but his voice was being drowned out by the rumbling of the tank. However, even without it Ivan must have been deafened and momentarily stunned by the battle noise. That moment later proved very costly, leaving marks on his body and soul that would probably last forever.

In his regiment he was neither heroic nor even noticeably courageous. With his infantryman's resilience and relative composure he was like everybody else. For earlier combats, he had received three certificates of gratitude from the commander-in-chief and two Medals for Courage and thought that he was not capable of more. And it had not been until he found himself there, in captivity, with no one to inspire him to feats of soldiering, reward him or even notice heroics, in danger of paying with his life for every small failure, that someone recalcitrant, defiant and stubborn was born inside of him. There he saw the underside of Nazism and understood, probably for the first time, that death was not the worst thing that could happen during the war.

"You give him *Brot?*" Giulia's voice suddenly echoed over him.

Ivan instinctively recoiled at the unexpected sound. However, the realisation that she had returned thrilled him, and he quickly turned around.

"You give him *Brot?*" Giulia kept asking with suppressed concern on her face. "We *non* Trieste? *Alles finito?* Yes?"

"Of course not!" he said and smiled. "I only gave him a crust."

She scrunched up her forehead and looked at him intensely. He took the last piece out of his pocket.

"Here. Just the crust. Understand?"

Giulia kept silent, battling something inside of her. Her forehead, however, was gradually smoothing out.

"We go Trieste? Truth? *Non?*"

"Of course we'll go. What made you think we wouldn't?"

Her face still reflected some struggle. Fingering the coat on her chest, the girl was probably making some decision. All of a sudden she threw herself to the ground where he was sitting. Pulling up her knees, she rested her hands on them and hid her face in her sleeves.

"*Russo.* You *gut Russo,*" she began to speak and squeezed his hand. "*Non* Vlasov. *Buono so.* Giulia bad."

"Oh, please," Ivan objected, suddenly embarrassed by her words. "It makes no sense. Stop it."

"Very, very," she kept saying without listening to him. Some pain within her must have subsided after the sudden explosion, she must have understood something over the torturous hour of their separation, and now she asked, "Ivan *non böse* Giulia? *Non böse?*"

"No, it's all right."

Sitting on the ground, he carefully took her small soft palm into his hands. Giulia did not withdraw it.

"*Non böse* Ivan," she said and looked into his eyes. "*Non böse* Giulia. Ivan know truth. Giulia *non* know truth."

"Oh, come on, please don't."

"Giulia very respect Ivan, love Ivan," she said.

His hands with her palm between them twitched ever so slightly.

"You, er, do you want a drink? Water?"

"Water? *Acqua?*"

"Yes, water," he brightened up. "Looks like there's a stream over there. *Ayda?*"

He quickly jumped to his feet. She also rose, clasped his arm above the elbow and pressed her cheek against it. He touched her hair with the other hand, stroked her, but then hurriedly lowered his arm, feeling that something inside of her had tensed. And so, having restored their peace and friendship, the two of them slowly started along the edge of the meadow.

19.

The brook was shallow and loud—the wide stream of icy mountain water was rushing furiously over the stones, whirling, foaming, sweeping over its low banks. Having crossed a wide bar of grey sand on the grass—a deposit along one of the stream's curves—Ivan and Giulia scooped up water in both hands and drank to their hearts' content. Giulia returned to the bank, while Ivan rolled up his dog-torn trousers and went deeper. His legs began to ache from the cold. The rapid current was pulling him off his feet, but he wanted to wash himself to get the stinging sweat off his face. Ivan felt his rough jaw and rather noticeable beard and tried to see himself in the water, but nothing was visible in the roiling sediment except stones and foam. *I must be scruffy as a thug,* he thought and looked back at Giulia.

"I'm ugly unshaven?" he asked Giulia, but she did not reply. Deep in thought, she continued to sit and look fixedly at the bank. "Am I ugly? Like an old man?"

She started, strained her ears, trying to read his mind, and then guessed as he kept picking at his stubbled jaws.

"*Gut,* Ivan. Very *wunderschön.*"

Ivan began to wash and thought that something must have happened to Giulia—she appeared anxious and distressed. She had not been so focused even under the Germans' noses. Such thoughtfulness was entirely out of character for her. It was he, Ivan, who had caused her some sort of distress. Unlike her, he forgot all his past anxieties and literally came back to life at that meadow feast of freedom. He felt good with her and wanted to dispel her anxiety and see her the way she had been before—cheerful, adventurous, trustful. He probably had to soothe and calm her, but, in spite of himself, Ivan could not cross a certain boundary between them. An impatient attraction to the girl was waking up within him, and yet it was restrained, painfully slow to take over his heart.

He finished washing, filled his cupped hands with water and swung them towards her—Giulia gave another start, looked at him in puzzlement and immediately smiled at his prank. His broad face, covered with curly stubble, also broke into an unaccustomed smile.

"Afraid?"

"*Non.*"

"Then why are you quiet?"

"Yes."

"What do you mean by 'Yes'?

"Yes," she said submissively. "Ivan yes, Giulia yes."

Despite bearing some burden on her heart, she was willingly yielding to his humour and watching him with a smile and a squint as he waddled towards her place on the grass, leaving wet prints in the sand with his bare feet.

"You're learning our language fast," he said as he recalled their recent conversation. "You must have been bright at school."

"Oh, I was *Wunderkind,*" Giulia said jokingly and gave a sudden start. Fear flashed across her face. "Oh, *Santa Madonna, il sangue!*"

"What?"

"*Il sangue! Blut!* Blut!"

Ivan bent over and glanced at his leg. A narrow trickle of blood was oozing from his knee down his wet shin. He immediately guessed that the wound caused by the dog had reopened. The injury was by no means serious—he had not yet even had time to examine it. Now he sat down next to the girl and rolled the trouser leg up higher. Indeed, a dog's claw had left nasty scratches above his knee, and contact with water had probably restarted the bleeding. Giulia swept towards him in fear, as if he had suffered some horrible injury.

"Oh, *Ivanio, Ivanio!* Hurt much? Hurt? Oh, *Madonna!* Where get such hurt?" she babbled and fussed.

"Why, from a dog," Ivan said with a chuckle. "I choked him, and he scratched me."

"*Santa Madonna!* Dog!"

Her nimble fingers began feeling his leg and wiping off fresh and already dry streaks of blood. He did not resist—sitting back, he yielded to her tender care. The experience was acutely sweet and surprisingly expansive. And yet blood was still seeping from the scratch, the edges of the wound had parted and would not stick together. His leg did not hurt at all, but it had to be bandaged.

Giulia rose slightly on her knees and ordered, "Look *nach montagna***. Nach montagna.*"

Realising that he had to turn away, Ivan obediently turned his face back towards the mountain. She tore something off her clothes. When he turned his head back, there was a clean scrap of calico in her hands.

---

*   *Sangue! Blut!* – blood (Italian and German)

**   *Nach montagna* – towards the mountain (German and Italian)

"*Medicamento* necessary. *Medicamento,*" she said, preparing to dress his wound.

"Come on, what medication? It'll heal like a dog wound."

"No, such hurt very bad."

"Wound, not hurt. In Russian it's wound."

"Wound, wound. Wound bad."

He looked around and, noticing the grey fringe of a ribwort-like grass, tore off several leaves.

"Here's a medication. Mother always used it."

"Dis? Dis is *plantago major. Non medicamento,*" she said and took the leaves out of his hands.

"Oh, come on! This is ribwort. Great for healing wounds."

"*Non* ribwort. Dis is *plantago major* in *latino.*"

"Aah, in Latin. Where did you learn it?"

Giulia gave him a playful glance.

"Giulia know *latino* much, much. Giulia *botanica* learn."

Ivan had also studied botany in the past, but now, unable to remember anything of that science and more reliant on custom, he pressed the ribwort leaves to his swollen scratch. The girl shook her head in disagreement but started dressing his foot with the white rag. Perhaps for the first time, Ivan felt her superiority—she probably had far more schooling than he did, and that made him respect her even more. Ivan cared little about his wound—he was more interested in the names of flowers. Reaching sideways, he plucked out a plant that looked very much like a daisy.

"What's this?"

She looked at the flower briefly. "*Pyrethrum roseum.*"

"No, nothing like our name. We'd probably call it a daisy."

He plucked out one more plant, a small and modest one, like a faded blue cornflower.

"And this?"

"Dis? Dis *primula auriculata.*"

"And this?

"*Gentiana pyrenaica,*" she said, taking two small blue funnel-shaped flowers on a rough leafy stem out of his hands.

"You know everything. Good for you. Only in Latin."

In the meantime Giulia applied some sort of dressing to his wound—two red stains immediately appeared on the cloth.

"Lie still necessary. Quiet necessary," she demanded.

Treating her anxiety with some playful indulgence, Ivan stretched out his leg and lay down on his side with his face towards her. Giulia drew up her legs and placed a hand on his heated shin.

"*Gut, Russo. Gut,*" she said, stroking his leg with care.

"You're saying I'm good but you don't believe me. You called me a Vlasovist," Ivan noted reproachfully, recalling their recent conflict.

She sighed and said judiciously, "Non Vlasovist. Giulia believe, Ivanio know truth. Giulia *non* understand truth."

Ivan looked long and hard into her strict eyes.

"And what did that Vlasovist tell you? Where did you hear him?"

"Camp hear," Giulia replied readily. "Vlasovist say: *Russo* kolkoz hunger, kolkoz bad."

Ivan smiled.

"He's a real scumbag. Probably a kulak. Of course, there were ups and downs. It wasn't such a paradise as you think. To be honest, I didn't want to tell you everything, but. . ."

"Talk, Ivan, truth! Talk!" Giulia asked persistently.

He plucked out a daisy and also sighed.

"There were bad harvests. But there were also different kolkhozes. And the soil wasn't the same everywhere. We, for example, had nothing but stones. And swamps for good measure. Of course, we would have done something about the soil one day. Look how many swamps we drained. Tractors appeared in the village. Different machines. Great help for working men. But the war blew everything to hell."

Giulia moved closer to him.

"Ivan talk Siberia. Giulia tink Ivan joke."

"No, why, there was Siberia too. Kulaks, those who were rich, were exiled. Enemies of different kinds were picked up as well. Our Tsyareshki also turned out to have four."

"Enemy? Why enemy?"

"They supported the bourgeois. Tried to infect kolkhoz cows with the disease we call glanders."

"Oh, oh! What bad mans!"

"There you have it. But maybe not all of them. Still, they were given ten years each. There had to be a reason. So they were also sent to Siberia. To reform."

"Truth?"

"Yes, what else could it be?"

Lying on his side, he was busily picking petals off the daisy.

"Ivan love his country very much?" Giulia asked after a short silence. "Bielorussia? Siberia? Your *gut* people?"

"Why, who else should I love? It was tough when Father died. We lived on potatoes. One village woman would bring us something, then another. Our neighbour Apanas would bring us firewood. Until I grew up. But there were bastards, too. There were people who reported our teacher Anatol Yauhenyevich, and, well, destroyed him. An honest man. He used to fight with the kolkhoz chief over mismanagement.

He cared about people. And yet he was accused of speaking against authorities. He also got ten years. By mistake, of course."

"Why honest teacher *non difendere*?"

"We did. Wrote. But. . ."

Ivan did not finish. Those involuntary recollections brought sad thoughts to his mind, and he lay, biting the stripped daisy stem. Anxious and attentive, Giulia was quietly stroking his bandaged hot knee.

"We saw it all. Old things were broken and rebuilt—we paid heavily for it. With blood. And yet difficulties are quickly forgotten, good things are remembered. Sometimes it seems that none of this happened. Our life was hard, troublesome, maybe unfair at times. But peaceful. And that's the most important thing. I sometimes think: let it all come back, both the difficulties and the hunger, but without war. We would cope with everything. We certainly would, after so much blood."

"*Russo fenomeno. Paradiso. Incredibile,*" Giulia started excitedly.

Ivan interrupted her, spitting out the stem.

"What's so incredible? It was a struggle. We lived under siege, surrounded by the bourgeois world, developed the Red Army."

"Oh, *armata Russo* win!" Giulia picked up.

"There you have it. That's how strong we've got. And oh if we used that strength for work after the war!"

"Giulia hear about Russia much. Russia—biggest justice." She kept silent for a while and then shifted her eyebrows, apparently recalling something. "Giulia for dis idea from *Vater, il padre,* I mean, father, run. Rome *Vater vernissage*

---

*   *Difendere* – defend (Italian)

make—*firma giubileo,* was much guest, SD *Offizier* was. *Offizier* Russia visit. *Offizier* say: 'Russia bad, poor, Russia non *Kultur.*' Giulia say: 'Dis is lie. Russia gooder *Deutschland.*' *Offizier* say: '*Fräulein comunista?*' Giulia say: '*Non comunista,* truth speaker.' *Il padre* hit Giulia." She briefly touched her cheek. "Slap in Russian. Giulia run *vernissage,* run Mario Napoli. Mario was *comunista.* Giulia tink *Russo gut.* Camp Ivan run, Giulia run. *Russo* Ivan hero!"

"Oh, come on, what hero?" Ivan objected. "Just a soldier."

"*Non* just soldier! *Russo soldato*—hero. Most brave! Most strong! Most, most," Giulia gushed, searching for Russian words. Everything about her tone bespoke the pained sincerity of a faith that she was very reluctant to betray. "We see your hero in camp. We know your hero at *Ostfront.* We tink your *Vaterland* most strong, most just."

"And it is just," Ivan noted. "Factory workers, kolkhozniks started making people of themselves. I myself got trained as a tractor driver. And we had so many teachers. Also former peasants. It wasn't like that in the past."

Her furrowed eyebrows moved and her eyes playfully flashed as some daring thought crossed her mind.

"*Russo comunista* Ivan save *Russland,* save bourgeois *monarchia Italiano,* save Giulia."

"Oh, come on, what Communist? That's too much honour. Besides, what's special about it? The entire Soviet Union is saving Italy, France and Greece. And God knows who else! Even though they are bourgeois. In fact, who could have stopped Hitler apart from us? Back then, in 1942?

"*Sì, sì.* Yes."

With a subtle smile on her lips, she swept her hand over his leg, then his bare side. Ivan literally froze at the gentle touch of her nimble, light fingers. Suddenly, she bent over and kissed the blue scar on his side. He shuddered, as if pierced with the bayonet for the second time, moved his hand to guard against her unrestrained tenderness, but she caught it, pulled it down and started kissing all his scars in one thoughtless impulse—a splinter scar on his shoulder, a bullet scar above his elbow, the bayonet scar on his side. She placed a careful peck on the bandage on his foot. He squinted from a terribly titillating sensation welling up inside him, tensed, and then his patience failed as he found a certain line in his ability to restrain himself to be too narrow to balance on. Not knowing whether that was good or bad but having already given way to an unknown force, he stirred and rose slightly on his elbows. He put his arm across her shoulder, pulled her a little closer, squeezed his eyes shut and touched her languid lips, feeling some unfamiliar flavour.

Then he immediately lay back on the grass, threw his arms apart and laughed, with his eyes still closed. And when he opened them and looked up, he saw her face and her open radiant white-toothed mouth in the sun's halo, under the veil of her loose hair. She seemed to choke up in that first second and looked eager but unable to say something. She simply stared at him, her eyes wide and round, and joy, bewilderment and happiness about her discovery surged into them from the depths of her heart, quickly overcoming embarrassment. The next second she nestled against his chest, snuggled up to him, hooked her hands around his neck and whispered with passion and devotion right next to his face, "Ivanio. . . *Amica. . .*"

20.

Something unfortunate and superfluous, a barrier that had been there all the time and kept them at a distance from each other, had been overcome, left behind happily and almost instantly. Giulia must have found some answer to the painful paradoxes that had troubled her—from that moment on, nothing existed for the two of them but the heady aroma of the soil, the scent of poppies and the heated radiance of the sky high above. Amid that primordial chaos, one step from death, something unknown, mysterious and powerful had been born. It was living, longing, frightening and beckoning.

Sprawled on the ground, Ivan stroked her warm narrow back again and again, while the girl kept pressing herself to his chest and rubbing her hot velvety cheek against his scarred shoulder. Her lips were incessantly whispering something unintelligible, foreign, but Ivan understood everything even without words. Laughing with his eyes, face and heart, he was seemingly frozen in some blissful weightlessness. The sky was spinning overhead. The Earth, like a huge lopsided plate, was tilting away and teetering, ready to plunge into an abyss, and he felt sweet, drunken and fearful.

Time must have ceased to exist for him, the danger passed into oblivion, two large black coals in her wide open eyes were smoldering hotly right next to his face. There was no longer any anguish, anxiety, or mischief in them, nothing except an urgent call, imperious in its muteness. Ivan had felt something like that while standing on the edge of a chasm, an invariably frightening and appealing experience. He had no strength whatsoever to resist that call, indeed, he did not know whether he should resist it. With his lips he once again found the moist liveliness of her mouth, felt the bony hardness of her teeth. The girl went silent and still, while he wrapped both arms around her and lay motionless. Everything became perfectly quiet, and the majestic mountain stream poured, rumbled and burbled into that quietude as if passing from non-existence into eternity. Ivan felt like dissolving, disappearing in her tremulous embrace, washing away into eternity with the stream, absorbing all the Earth's force and becoming that force himself—generous, quiet, gentle.

And the Earth was still teetering, the sky was spinning. Through his half-closed eyes he saw more closely than ever before the gentle swell of her cheek with small hairs highlighted by the sun. The slender backlit rim of her ear was shining a bright pink. He reached over to her earlobe with a barely visible hole in it and quietly felt it with his lips—Giulia jolted at his touch.

A unfamiliar and totally alien voice that had probably been awakened by her movement called out in confusion from somewhere in his heart—it was hesitant and resistant, afraid of something. It did not seem to have any arguments, compelling, irrefutable facts. The logic behind its reservations came down to a set of reproachful questions, *Why? Why? What are you doing? Do you know who she is? You know very little. No, you know nothing at all! Where is she from? Remember the world she's from?*

Ivan tried to ignore and muffle the skeptic within him. He did not want to know anything now—he felt the churning, splashing, roaring stream, the resonance of everything inside the Earth, and a persistent and powerful impulse in his heart echoing the Earth sound with a band of trumpets.

The Earth's axis must have tilted at that point, but Ivan was paying no attention—he was ready to plunge into the abyss, for nothing mattered now with Giulia in his arms. She was the ethereal and unknown one, lost in the dazzling riot of poppy reds, subdued, small, weakened and therefore vested with even more power—over the Earth, over herself, over him.

A furious stream seemed to be roaring, racing and gushing just beneath them, deep in the bowels of the Earth. It was pulling and luring Ivan into its unexplored depths, and he no longer had the strength to resist it. She started flopping and splashing like a fish in his arms. Strange, familiar and very understandable words were forming and dying on her wide open lips.

But words did not matter now.

The bowels of the Earth, the mountains and the mighty anthems of all the streams of the Earth went still and unanimously blessed the great mystery of life.

21.

He woke up suddenly, with an anxiously joyous effort of will, startled by the thought that he had fallen asleep and allowed something exceedingly great and blissful to disappear from his life.

With his head slightly raised, he instantly took in his surroundings and immediately broke into a smile, realising that his fear had been unfounded—nothing had disappeared, gone missing or even turned out to have been a dream. For the first time in many years of his life, reality was better than the happiest dream.

Giulia lay prone in the grass with her cheek resting quietly on her outstretched hand, asleep. However, she was not breathing rhythmically and evenly the way sleeping people do—she occasionally went still, as if straining to hear something, exhaled and then took some even short breaths and let them out with restrained joy. Her slightly parted lips were moving all the time. At first he thought that she was whispering, but no words came out. Her lips appeared to be simply reflecting the mysterious events of her dreams, just like her cheeks and eyelids. Even in her sleep they moved and twitched. And yet all emotions evoked by her dream were sweet and peaceful—she seemed to be dreaming about something cheerful, and a kind, subtle smile appeared on her lips from time to time.

Ivan rolled over on his side and sat up. They must have been lying there for a long time. The sun had already slipped off the horizon and was setting behind the darkened hump of the twin summits. The meadow, so solemnly bright during the day, looked very humble and almost inhospitable without sunlight. There was a dense shroud of fog in the distance, and although clouds were not in sight, a bleak foggy mist had eroded the distant mountain ridges and completely flooded the valley. The bear's ridge had lost its wooded foothills and, still glittering with its silvery summits, was floating in the smoky sea of fog like a melting iceberg. That was the last parting gleam of light at the end of that extraordinary, unanticipated and rewarding day for Ivan. A solitary star had already lit up on the faded horizon and was quietly shining in the distance.

He turned towards Giulia again. They probably had to get up and walk, but she was sleeping so sweetly, so helplessly and exhaustedly that he simply did not dare disturb her much-needed rest. He started longingly watching her face, animated even in sleep, as if he had never seen it before. After all that had happened between them, her every smiling feature, every movement took on its own deeper significance. He felt like watching her all eternity, exploring with his senses the alluring mystery of the human heart. Contrary to everything, he had discovered something unexpectedly modest and joyful in her and nearly suffocated from that first rush of heady excitement. By now, the excitement had worn off a little, but the feeling of happiness had actually grown stronger, and the skeptical voice within him had fallen silent forever. All in all, it had been simply foolish to have dithered for so long, to have ever had doubts about this purest and probably most unselfish of all creatures in the world. Now that he had understood that truth, he sat motionless, watching Giulia like a wonderful mystery of nature, never taking his eyes off the small human miracle he had discovered so belatedly and joyfully. He felt neither contempt nor disgust for that girl from the West. There was only something quiet and kind causing his heart to overflow with tenderness.

She was still asleep, nestled against the broad chest of the Earth. Her thin nostrils were moving and trembling, and a small red ladybird was crawling dreamily along her sleeve. It had emerged from a fold, spread its wings and then apparently decided against flying and simply crawled on. He carefully removed the ladybird, reached up to the girl's neck and cautiously adjusted the small cross on a twisted black string. She held her breath briefly but did not wake up, and so he smoothed out a folded edge of the coat on her back and smiled. Who could have thought that in two days she would become what none of his compatriots had ever been, that she would captivate his heart at that seemingly least suitable moment? Could Ivan have foreseen that he would meet his first love so unexpectedly, on the run for the fourth time, fleeing from death? How tangled, twisted and confused the world had become! Or else how would that have happened—in captivity, on the threshold of death, with a strange, unknown girl, a person from another world? *What would the lads say if they learnt such details?* he wondered, and the thought made him uncomfortable. The question was not simple to say the least, but Ivan did not have to be taught how to be straight with himself. He easily pictured the stern, displeased face of Golodai—he would probably not allow any romance. Golodai always knew what he wanted and never wavered in his intentions.

Zhuk was unlikely to praise him either, for he harboured too much anger against the Krauts to tolerate some silly romance on the way to revenge. Yanushka would probably be too sensitive to scold him. He would try to put everything down to his youth, but in his heart he would also condemn Ivan rather than justify him. The wretched Srebnikau would not forgive him either, but for a different reason. And yet, although he also was no softy, coward or weakling, Ivan had given in, fallen in love with the little Alpine miracle that had so unexpectedly proven more important and valuable than anything else in his life.

Still, they had to go. *We shouldn't be lying around relaxing now, I'd better wake her up,* he thought and lay down next to her, tight against her side but careful not to disturb her sleep. Overcome by tenderness, he drew dangling poppy stems away from her face and chased away a fluttering white moth which kept trying to land on her hair. *Let her sleep a little longer,* Ivan thought, still trying to make himself comfortable. *Just a little—and we must go. Down into the valley.*

The broad bear's ridge was quietly fading in the subdued sky over the foggy jumble of mountains. The grey twilight was climbing higher and higher over its steep sides, and the rosy glitter on the pointed summits was fading.

Soon it was gone completely. The ridge immediately shrank and sagged, a grey mist enveloped the mountains, and the first stars broke out on the grey sky. Ivan, however, did not see them. His last thought before he fell asleep was that he had to get up.

This time he was the one who was woken up. Probably getting cold, Giulia began to stir next to him, snuggling closer against his side. Ivan was still sleepy, but he immediately felt her touch and gave a start. Giulia put her arm around him. With deep passion, she began to whisper into his ear words that were full of tenderness—strange, alien words that were very dear to him. He pulled her closer and met her lips with his.

The darkness became complete. The temperature dropped. The black humps of the nearer summits loomed on the horizon, filling half the sky. A handful of stars were twinkling overhead. The wind must have died down, for even the poppies were not rustling. Only the rumbling, bubbling sounds of the nearby stream were unfaltering and steady. The night brought out all the fragrance of the profusion of grasses in the meadow, injecting a slight drunkenness into his blood. The Earth, the mountains and the night sky were dozing with a quiet confidence. Ivan rose slightly, leaned towards the girl and took a long look at her. Serene like the night itself, subdued and seemingly a little scared, her face was not the same as during the day. The obscured pupils were moving in her huge eyes, and each of them had a barely visible star glittering in its distant depth. Vague night shadows were drifting over her face, and her hands kept stroking and caressing his shoulders, neck and the back of his head, never losing their sensuous liveliness even at night.

"Giulia!" he called softly, still holding her tight.

"*Ivanio?*" she responded obediently—in a quiet voice full of tenderness and devotion.

"You are not afraid of me?"

"No, *Ivanio.*"

"That I will cheat and leave you?"

"*Non, amica.* Ivan *non* cheat. Ivan—*Russo. Gut,* dear *Russo!*"

With a hasty energetic movement and surprising strength for her slender arms, she pressed Ivan to herself and gave a soft happy chuckle.

"Ivan *marito**. *Non signore* Giangarini, *non* Mario. *Russo* Ivan *marito*."

"And you? Are you happy? Won't you regret that Ivan—*marito?*" he asked with satisfaction and even secret pride in his heart.

Shaded by his head, her eyes went wide open, and the stars in her pupils twitched and began to dance.

"Ivan—*gut, gut marito*. We will small, small *figlio*. How is das Russian?"

"Child?"

"*Non* child! How is dat small *Russo?*"

"Aah, a son," he prompted, a little surprised.

"Yes, son! Dis is *gut*. Such small, small *gut* son. He will Ivan, yes?"

"Ivan? Well, why not?" he agreed and sighed, glancing over her shoulder at the black expanse of the distant ridge.

She went quiet, pondering something. Both of them were silent for a minute, each immersed in the world of their thoughts. All around them lay serene mountains. Sparsely scattered stars were gleaming with a faint glow. The poppy meadow was covered with an impenetrable black haze. Everything was perfectly still, only the stream was rushing and churning, but it did not disturb the silence, and Ivan felt that there was no one in the whole world but the two of them and the stream. However, there was an unsettling quality to her final words that chased away the smile from Ivan's face. Now his jocular lightness was gone, he stumbled upon

---

*　　　*Marito* – husband (Italian)

something troubling and serious in himself and, perhaps for the first time, saw one more twist in their highly complex relationship. Giulia, on the contrary, soon started at some joyful thought and squeezed him again in her embrace.

"*Ivanio! Ivanio gut!* How *gut* it is—*figlio,* son! Small son!"

Then she unclasped her hands and rolled over on her stomach. The stars in her eyes disappeared, and her face turned vaguely grey, a light stain in the grass with a barely visible flicker in the deep shadows of her eye sockets. Her momentary delight gave way to unexpected anxiety.

"*Ivanio,* and where we will live? *Roma?*" She thought for a second. "Non Rome. Rome *Vater böse.* Trieste?"

"Let's not get ahead of ourselves," he said.

"Oh!" she suddenly gave a soft cry. "Giulia know. We will live Russia. Bielorussia. Village Tsyareshki, two lakes very close. Yes?"

"Maybe. Why?"

All of a sudden, she recalled something and grew alert.

"Tsyareshki kolkoz?"

"Kolkhoz, Giulia. Why?"

"Ivanio, kolkoz bad?"

"Never mind. Things will get better one day. Bad things cannot go on forever."

With his big hand, he stirred her coarse thick hair, but she drew away and smoothed it.

"Hair will big. Giulia grow big, *gut* hair. Big *gut* hair beautiful, yes?"

"Yes," he agreed. "Beautiful."

She kept silent for a while and then said, picking up where she had left off, "Ivan will *lavorare* *farme, plantazione.*

---

*   *Lavorare* – work (Italian)

Giulia will. How is das? *Wirtin villa*[*]. We make many, many poppies. Like dis meadow!"

"Yes, yes," Ivan kept nodding thoughtfully, stirring on the ground.

His leg stung sharply under the dressing. The cloth probably had to be adjusted, but he did not want to disturb her now. He simply straightened out his leg and positioned it more comfortably on the grass. Deep in thought, he was listening to Giulia's sincere and soulful words, full of tenderness and hope.

"We will many, many *fortuna*[**]. I want *fortuna* very much. Man should be *fortuna*. Truth, Ivanio?"

"Yes, yes."

She was clearly fighting sleep, her voice was becoming increasingly soft and sleepy, and she soon fell silent. Ivan gave her a quiet stroke and thought that he should probably let her rest, get enough sleep. Little was left of that night anyway, the first night of their happiness. And in the morning they would have to go. Only who knew what that morning had in store for them?

He watched the sky for a long time, one on one with the universe, with the hundreds of stars, large and barely visible, with the twisty road of the Milky Way right across the sky. A germ of alarm and anxiety began to displace his short-lived happiness.

Over the war years, he had completely forgotten what it meant to seek happiness, a perfectly simple human aspiration. What happiness could you possibly pursue if you clutched at every straw to somehow survive and avoid

---

[*]   *Wirtin villa* – lady of the house (German and Italian)

[**]   *Fortuna* – good luck (Italian)

death, and the only way to succeed was to kill others? Even predators do not kill members of their own species, but the ruthless custom of destroying their own kind was the predominant method of struggle among humans. And what did they kill for? For material gain, for the domination of a beastly ideology, for the control of a tiny handful of people over others? May German Nazism be damned forever! Will your pack of wolves never understand that you cannot build your happiness upon the great misery of millions? By destroying others, you will be the first to be poisoned and lose your capacity for joy. The crimes you commit will smother your heart with the foul blackness of hatred. This is the rich inheritance you want to pass on to your heirs. But will they want to take this inheritance from your bloody hands? Will they also not want the sun of justice and peace to shine after the night of the stench of death in which you have kept the world for the past ten years?

Fortunately, the feast of "those predators" would soon be over, happiness would eventually prevail. In due course, people would discover the great privilege of love and devotion. For them, however, there was probably no such hope. Dear, good-hearted Giulia, she flies so far ahead in her dreams, apparently unaware of anything that awaits them on their way to Trieste. After breaking out of the camp and experiencing love in that wondrous poppy paradise, she must have assumed that everything dreadful was now behind them and only joy lay ahead. If only that were true! A moment's reflection made it clear how much suffering lay ahead—highways in the valley that were very difficult to cross, rivers that God alone knew how to ford, villages that could not be avoided. And what about people, ambushes, dogs? To cap it all, there was the inaccessible snowy ridge! How could they cross it without clothes, footwear and food?

Giulia, however, continued to sleep quietly on her side, with her leg bent at the knee. Ivan got up, scanned the terrain, walked around her and sat down again, dejected and angry. He was very hungry, but the worst thing was the pain in his leg. His shin seemed to be getting thicker and thicker, and the dressing was really tight. Ivan loosened it a little and felt around—his leg was on fire, and shivers were setting in. He had to pick up the hateful striped coat from the grass and wrap it around himself. Alas, even the coat was not warm enough. More attentive to himself now, Ivan thought how inappropriate it would be to fall ill. What would happen then? *No, enough of that!* he reassured himself. *Hang on!*

However, something about Ivan's mood had changed, and anxiety was welling up in his heart like water in a leaky boat. Fortunately, Giulia was sleeping soundly and probably feeling no threat. He sat down beside her, wrapped an edge of his coat around his bare feet and started looking into the night. He soon grew sleepy, distracted only by the steady bubbling of the stream.

The day must have begun to dawn when he dropped his guard and dozed off unconsciously, pressing his face to his knees.

22.

Dulled by slumber, his anxiety came back with a sudden jolt, which seemed to strike straight at his heart. It flipped so violently that his chest nearly burst open. He started and instantly heard a senseless, mad scream.

"*Wo bist du, Russe? Sie Brot geben. Sie haben viele Brot.*"[*]

The day was gradually dawning over the meadow, the sun had not yet risen, and the landscape was inhospitable and grey. A cloud must have crept over the mountains, for they were now invisible. A swirling sliver of fog was crawling along the slope, catching on drooping dewy poppy plants. Ivan immediately yanked the jacket from Giulia's feet. She jerked and started babbling in fear, while he was standing on all fours and looking downhill, towards the source of the noise. In a few seconds, he realised that the madman was back. However, he immediately sensed that the *Häftling* was not alone—there were people with him. Indeed, before he had seen anyone through the fog, he heard a muffled threatening voice, "*Halt's Maul!*"[**] and typical German swearing.

Giulia, who had also heard the noise and understood everything, threw herself towards Ivan. Clutching at his coat

---

[*]   *Wo bist du, Russe? Sie Brot geben. Sie haben viele Brot* - Where are you, Russian? They give bread! They have a lot of bread. (German)

[**]   *Halt's Maul!* – shut your mouth! (German)

sleeve, she was staring downhill at the smoky mishmash of fog where they had glimpsed something like human shadows. He grabbed her hand, hunched and dragged her towards the stream, to lower ground. He was holding the leather jacket in the other hand. Her clogs had been left somewhere in the poppy field.

Without a word they ran upstream as fast as they could.

Ivan was flying along, jumping over stones, never letting go of Giulia's fingers. The girl was barely keeping up with him and constantly looking back in fear. Ivan was searching for a convenient place to cross the stream and hide among the rocks and the tall and dense rhododendron shrubs on the other side. But the stream was rushing down from the mountains, gathering speed along the way, and did not look crossable. It would be hopeless trying to wade through it.

Thank God for the cloud! Thank God for the cloud! Ivan thought, the words pounding in his head. The fast-flowing wisps of fog were providing some cover from the Germans, who were very close. *The damned madman, why didn't I kill him? They're all cut from the same cloth, both sane and mad. Betrayed again. Maybe for the last time?* Ivan wondered in despair as he mercilessly dragged Giulia along without releasing her hand. They had already left the curve of the stream behind, reached the bank and were about to enter a clear space. Before dashing out into the open dewy meadow, Ivan dropped to his knees, then rose slightly, panting, and looked down. The fog had become noticeably thinner, the distant stones among the poppies and the knoll where he had met the madman the previous day had already come into view. And then he saw several Germans through the foggy air—they had fanned out across the meadow and were approaching the knoll in a narrow chain.

The Germans could not yet see them. The fugitives had run quite a long way and put some distance between themselves and their pursuers. Ivan glanced at Giulia. There was great weariness on her lively face, which bore traces of sleep, her breathing was so laboured that she was almost suffocating. *Please, keep her going! Please, keep her going!* Ivan thought desperately, for only their own feet could save them now. And so, after taking a few breaths, he pulled her by the hand again. Giulia was obviously running with tremendous difficulty, and yet she was keeping up with him.

Panting loudly, their legs wet to the knees with dew, they had already left the middle of the meadow far behind. Alas, their pace got slower with every minute. Ivan developed a pronounced limp, his right leg was surprisingly unresponsive, as if he had sat on it for too long. He thought at first that it had gone numb during his slumber, but the uncontrollable weakness persisted, and a tendon under his knee knotted up. It was not long before Giulia noticed his limp and pulled at his arm in alarm.

"*Ivanio*, foot?"

He dragged it over the grass, trying to make his step as natural as possible, but he did poorly. Giulia looked back and then threw herself down on her knees and grabbed his trouser leg, intending to examine the wound.

"Necessary bind, yes? A little bind?"

He resolutely moved her arms away.

"Forget it, let's go faster."

"Hurt, yes? Hurt?" she kept asking with a suppressed anxiety in her huge eyes, peering inquiringly at him. Her chest under her striped coat was heaving violently from exhaustion. Her coarse eyebrows were raised above her eyes and twitching nervously.

"It's nothing, nothing."

He hobbled on, defying pain as he scrambled uphill. Giulia's hand slipped out of his fingers, but he did not retrieve it—she was running alongside him, looking back all the time.

"*Ivanio, amica,* we will live? Will we?" she was asking with heartrending despair.

Ivan looked back at her, not knowing what to say, but saw so much pleading and hope in her eyes that he hastened to lie, "Of course we will. But let's run faster."

"*Ivanio,* I faster. I fast. I *gut.*"

"Good, good."

They had already reached the upper part of the meadow. The path that had brought them there at night began somewhere among the stones. The mountains and the rocks could probably give them shelter. By now, however, the cloud must have cleared the meadow. The daylight grew even brighter, the fog was thinning by the minute, and flashing patches of poppies and stones could now be seen with perfect clarity through breaks in the foggy veil. *Damn, won't we get away?* he thought, the words throbbing in his mind. *Will they see us? No, this shouldn't happen!* Ivan kept reassuring himself as he climbed higher. An experienced fugitive, he understood all the gravity of their situation and knew that they were unlikely to escape if they were spotted by the Germans.

However, the path was nowhere to be seen, and they simply continued to climb the grassy meadow slope. Luckily, the rise was not steep. Their only hindrance were the low rhododendron shrubs, which left numerous cuts on their bare feet. But trailing coniferous shrubs where they could hide were not far ahead. He should not have been afraid that Giulia would fall behind. With her bare feet bleeding, she was actually slightly ahead of him, and every time she looked back, he saw her face, which expressed a kind of determination to escape misfortune he had never noticed throughout their journey from the camp. Neither stones on the ground, nor fatigue, nor pricks and thorns seemed to be getting in her way now—like a tigress, she appeared ready to fight tooth and nail to survive.

"*Ivanio!* Fast! Fast!"

She was urging him forward now! Ivan clenched his teeth at that thought—with his leg growing heavier and heavier, his own fortunes seemed to be declining. He surreptitiously pulled up his trouser leg and immediately lowered it. His knee had swollen and turned blue and thick as a log. *What the hell is this? Can this be inflammation?*

Meanwhile, as if by an unlucky coincidence, the last wisps of the cloud sailed past and the meadow turned a muted red. And immediately three gloomy, stone-like figures floated out of the fog one by one. Eight or so of them were walking tiredly across the meadow, trampling flowers and peering uphill.

There was no point in hiding any longer.

Ivan sat down, throwing the jacket to the ground. The dejected and apparently confused Giulia stopped nearby. For several seconds, they were so short of breath that they could not say a word and simply watched their pursuers. The Germans, however, immediately began to talk. One of them was pointing an outstretched hand at the fugitives, and the commander barked an order. The striped figure of a man was plodding in the middle of the chain. His hands seemed to be tied behind his back, and two escorts pushed him in the shoulders when he stopped. That was probably the madman.

The Germans began to move faster and then dashed uphill with shouts.

"All right then," Ivan said. "Just don't be afraid. Don't. Let them come!.."

He put on the jacket to free his hands and took the pistol out of his pocket. Giulia, now downhearted and silent, seemed to have turned to stone. The narrow gap between her eyebrows closed, and a look of resolute stubbornness came over her face like a shadow.

"All right, let's go. And let them run—they'll get tired."

"Will *schiessen?*" Giulia said in surprise, as if she had just understood the danger they were facing.

"It's too far. Let them shoot if they have extra cartridges."

Indeed, the Germans were not shooting yet, they were just shouting their "*Halt!*" but the fugitives hurried uphill, towards the shrubs. Giulia had already overcome her initial confusion and become her nimble and risky self and appeared ready for anything.

"Let them *schiessen!* I *non* afraid. Let *schiessen!*" the girl kept saying.

Looking back all the time, she jumped close to Ivan and took his hand. He gratefully squeezed her cold fingers and kept them in his fist.

"*Ivanio*, SS *Offiziers*—we *schiessen!* We *non* camp, no?"

He anxiously knitted his brows.

"Of course. Just don't be afraid."

"I *non* afraid. *Russo non* afraid—Giulia *non* afraid."

He was not afraid. He had felt fear too often over the war years to be scared now. As soon as he saw the Germans, he immediately became calm and collected, full of determination and agility. His only wish was that God would give strength to both him and Giulia. A suppressed anxiety for her was gnawing at his heart. He had stifled all other feelings—they would be unnecessary and harmful now. From now on he would rely on the animal instincts of a fighter. A battle of agility, cunning and speed was beginning. They had to run and save their energy, stay out of gunshot range and fight their way to the clouds, which had lain motionless over the mountaintops since nightfall. That was the only way to go. They had no other options.

23.

They finally reached the shrubs but did not try to hide—they no longer needed shelter. Dislodging sand and debris with their feet, clutching at prickly branches, Giulia got to the top of the cliff ahead of him and stopped. Ivan was climbing behind her, raising his injured leg sideways. So bad was the pain in his knee that he simply did not know how to climb the steep patch near the very top. Seeing that, the girl knelt down and held out her thin weak hand to him. He looked at the blue streaks of veins on her wrist and moved her hand away—how could she possibly cope with his weight? But Giulia began to jabber in a strange mixture of Italian, German and Russian and urgently grabbed him under the elbow, supporting him as best she could, and he eventually dragged his ponderous bulk over the edge.

"Fast, Ivan, fast! SS!"

Indeed, the Germans were closing in. The ones in front had already crossed the meadow and were climbing the cliff, the others were catching up with them. The madman in striped clothes was stumbling behind everybody else with his hands bound, accompanied by an escort. Someone at the front saw them near the shrubs, shouted and fired one burst from an assault rifle. The shots cracked through the morning air, echoing loudly in the distant ravines. Ivan looked back. The Germans were quite far away, and he did not hear the sound of bullets. And when he started forward again, he almost bumped into Giulia who was lying on the slope.

"What's wrong?"

"*Non, non! Non erschiessen**!" she said, looking back with a joyous sparkle in her eyes, and jumped to her feet. Her face was radiating a vivacious, mischievous excitement. "Bastards SS!" she shouted at the Germans in a ringing indignant voice. "*Verfluchter Schwein!*** *Nichts erschiessen*, hey!"

"All right, enough of that!" Ivan said.

They had to save their energy, what was the use of teasing those predators? But Giulia's anger and long-standing bitterness seemed to have got the better of her, and she was clearly reluctant to simply flee.

"Hitler *kaputt!* Hitler *cretino!* Come on, *schiessen*, come on!"

The Germans fired some more bursts, but the fugitives were on much higher ground than the pursuers and, Ivan knew, almost unreachable to assault rifles. Giulia must have also sensed their advantage, and the fact that not a single bullet had zinged around them set her on fire with malicious mischief.

"Come on, *schiessen! Schiessen*, come on! *Fascisti! Briganti!****"

She was red from tiredness and indignation, her eyes were burning with a malevolent black light, her close-cropped thick hair was ruffling in the wind. At the end of her tirade, she grabbed a stone from under her feet, swung

---

*   *Erschiessen* – shoot dead (German)

**   *Verfluchter Schwein!* – damned pig!(German)

***   *Briganti!* – bandits! (Italian)

it awkwardly and flung it downhill. Bouncing, it rolled far away into the distance.

Ivan was now in the lead. They were clambering along the edge of the thicket, over increasingly steep terrain. Those goddamn shrubs, they would have been welcome there, at the bottom, where it was still possible to hide. Now, however, they were simply getting in the way, prickling their feet and tripping them up. But he was afraid of scrambling right through them, so densely intertwined were their twisted wire-like resinous branches. Again and again, he glanced upwards with anxiety, looking for a more convenient path, but saw no better way to go. All he could do was stifle his dismay. Looming above them was another cliff, much taller than the previous one, crumbling, probably impossible for them to climb.

Giulia, however, seemed to see and feel nothing. Preoccupied with the Germans, she fell behind a little and then hurried to catch up with him. He sat down, panting, and stretched out his bad leg.

"*Ivanio,* foot?" she looked up at him in fear.

He made no reply.

"Foot? Give foot!"

He rose silently and took another look at the cliff. Her gaze grew anxious when she also looked in that direction and examined the wall of stone.

"*Ivanio!*"

"All right. Let's go."

"*Ivanio!*"

Her face twitched again, as if from pain, she looked back and saw the Germans scrambling uphill, following in their footsteps.

"*Ivanio,* we will *morto**! *Non* Tsyareshki? *Alles non?*"

"Let's go faster! Faster!" he snapped at her without making a reply, for they had no choice but to cut across the shrubs.

And so Ivan bit his lip and plunged into the impenetrable growth, which even wild animals avoided. Hundreds of prickly needles immediately sunk into his feet, but he was paying no attention to them—he was sparing only his knee. A cold sweat broke out on his forehead forehead from pain and tension. Taking no real precautions but mustering every ounce of his endurance, he was climbing like crazy among the shrubs, working his way sideways to bypass the cliff.

"Ouch, ouch! Ouch!" Giulia was yelping in despair and yet climbing after him, not very deft or intentional about where she was going, frequently getting stuck in thorns and falling.

He was neither comforting her nor urging her forward— he was just looking back at the edge of the cliff where the Germans were bound to appear at any moment.

This time, however, they were lucky. They had almost reached the upper part of the thicket when the first SS officer came into view. He was now becoming dangerous, for although Ivan and Giulia were at a distance from him, they had not climbed high enough, and the altitude difference was small. As soon as the German raised his head to see where they were, Ivan took aim and fired.

A loud echo rolled through the mountains.

Sure enough, the shot went wide. Although he was still quite a long way away, the German cautiously slipped under the cliff. And then the air erupted with a long staccato burst

---

*   *Morto* – dead (Italian)

of gunfire. *Ra-ta-ta-ta. Ra-ta-ta-ta. Ta-ta-ta. Ta-ta.* The mountains reverbated with the sound, multiplying it several times over. When the echo died down, the fugitives started running again. The unexpected pistol shot had apparently confused the Germans, for no one showed up at the top of the cliff for some time. Then a striped figure appeared at the edge.

"*Ivanio, Häftling!*"

Spreading his feet wide, the madman climbed the cliff and screamed, wobbling, in his ridiculously broken voice, "*Russe! Russe! Halt! Warum du gehst weg? Sie wollen Brot geben.**"

"*Zurück!***" Ivan shouted. "*Schiessen!*"

The madman hunched and beat a retreat. They heard the Germans shout at him, and then, after a brief wait, all of them to a man spilled out from under the cliff almost simultaneously.

Things seemed to be going from bad to worse. Although the saddle where the thicket ended was very close, they were now exposed to the Germans' assault rifles. Something had to be done to delay them and break through to the other side of the saddle. Ivan knelt, leaned the barrel of the pistol against a shaky branch and fired for the second time, then the third. Then he hunched and squatted down among low-growing shrubs. Giulia slipped over to him on all fours.

"Ivan, *non Patron alles!**** *Non alles!*"

---

*   *Russe! Russe! Halt! Warum du gehst weg? Sie wollen Brot geben* – Russian! Stop! Why are you going away? They want to give bread (German)

**   *Zurück!* – back! (German)

***   *non Patron alles!* – not all the cartridges!

Ivan reassuringly touched her slender shoulder—of course, he would leave two cartridges for the very end. He was expecting shots from the Germans, but they were silent. Having spread out over a wide area, they also entered the thicket. And so he jumped to his feet and hobbled uphill to the saddle near a cliff, hunching to be a little less exposed.

Still, the Germans must have made a mistake by following them into the shrubs. The thicket was not only hindering their progress but also blocking their view and preventing them from taking aim. They were still plodding along when Ivan and Giulia reached the saddle, barely alive from exhaustion.

With the last of their strength and expecting shots from behind with every body part, they ran over to it and then swept down to the other side like bullets. The first thing Ivan did after that was cast his gaze over the new horizon. A steep stony slope similar to the one behind their backs rose all the way to the low-hanging clouds on one side. The terrain under their feet descended abruptly into a ravine and then climbed to another low mountain ridge. Scattered here and there over the mountains, clouds were sailing in the sky, looking as white as a flock of sheep. A solid shroud of higher-level clouds covered the snowy mountaintops.

No sooner had they cleared the saddle than Giulia folded her hands on her chest, fell to her knees and started whispering something very quickly.

"What are you doing?" he shouted.

Without a reply, Giulia whispered some more words, and Ivan ran downhill, limping badly. She immediately jumped to her feet and caught up with him.

"*Santa Maria* will help. I ask very, very."

He was genuinely surprised.

"Come on! Who will help you? Let's hurry up!"

Not knowing where to go and too weak to climb uphill, they were running across the slope down to the ravine. The saddle and the cliff were still shielding them from the Germans. The downhill run was extremely easy—their bodies seemed to be running on their own, carrying them so fast that their knees buckled. Ivan, however, continued to limp, unable to do anything about his leg. Giulia was running ahead of him but keeping the distance between them short and looking back all the time. She seemed to be swelling with liveliness and some unrestrained excitement about their escape from under the Germans' noses. Casting daredevil looks over her shoulder, she was babbling words of hope and joy, "*Ivanio,* we will live! Live, *Ivanio!* I want live very much! *Bravo vita!*"

No, it's too early to celebrate, Ivan thought but did not argue, letting her have her way. He looked back as well and immediately saw the first SS officer appear in the saddle. The tall fellow in riding breeches held up by braces and an unbuttoned uniform revealing a white shirt on his chest climbed heavily into view. No, he was in no hurry to shoot, even though they were not very far from him and on much lower ground. For half a minute, he stood motionless, peering at them. Then he started saying something to those who were apparently coming up from behind and burst into laughter. He roared with laughter for a long time, shouting something to the fugitives, and finally sat down in the saddle calmly and took off his cap.

Giulia jumped over to Ivan and started shaking his sleeve.

"*Ivanio, Ivanio,* look! He *gut tedesco!* He let us go? Let us go! Let's go. Look!"

Ivan saw everything but had no idea why they had not been chased and shot at and why the Germans had left them alone and huddled together on the mountain. One of them stepped aside and started shouting, waving his assault rifle, "*Schneller! Schneller! Lauf schneller!*"

"*Ivanio,* they let us go!" Giulia babbled joyously as she ran. "We live, we live!"

Ivan was silent.

What the hell? What games are they playing? What are they going to do? His brain was almost exploding, unable to understand the enemy's new tricks. Their behaviour was really strange. But he knew that it was not accidental, that kind-heartedness was not the reason the Germans had abandoned their pursuit, that the enemies were up to something even worse.

But what was it?

They reached the very bottom of the ravine, scrambled through the rhododendrons to a low, gentle swell on the other side and began an exhausted climb. Sandy patches created by the wind and the thorns of the low-growing grass had turned their feet into raw flesh, but they no longer felt the hardness of the ground. Giulia would run forward and then return, looking back at the Germans at the top. The farther behind they left the saddle, the more cheerful she became. But in the end she could not help being dismayed by his dejected look.

"*Ivanio,* why *furioso?* Foot, yes?" she kept asking.

"No."

"Why? We will live, Ivanio. We escape."

---

*   *Lauf schneller!* – run faster! (German)

By that point, he had understood what was probably going on. Without answering her, Ivan was running lamely towards the top of the swell. Beyond it the terrain swung steeply downwards, potentially hiding them from the Germans. That was good, but. . .

They were near the top when Giulia seemed to grasp something too and stopped. The mountains ahead of them suddenly parted to reveal a broad expanse of blue air— below them lay a gloomy ravine with swirling, creeping tendrils of fog rising out of it.

They ran over to the cliff in silence and shrank back. The slope plunged precipitously into a misty abyss marked here and there with tongues of lingering snow.

24.

Giulia was lying on a stone ledge five steps away from the drop and weeping. Ivan did not try to comfort or calm his companion—he was sitting next to her with his hands propped on the rough mossy ground and thinking that that was probably going to be their end. There was an encroaching precipice up ahead and off to one side. On the other side, a rocky slope rose steeply all the way to the clouds. In the saddle behind them there were the Germans. They had found themselves in a perfect, most carefully laid trap. How on Earth did they manage to get so badly stuck? For Giulia, who had unexpectedly begun to hope for an escape, the discovery was particularly shocking and painful, and Ivan was not talking to her now—he had nothing to say.

Chilly damp air was rising from the abyss. Their heated bodies were beginning to cool. The wind was roaring through the surrounding rocks like smoke rushing through giant chimneys. It was cloudy and very uncomfortable. But why were the Germans not coming and shooting? Huddled together in the saddle above the fugitives, some of them were sitting, while others were standing around the striped figure of the *Häftling*. After a closer look, Ivan understood everything—they were having fun. They were smoking and sticking their cigarettes alternately at his forehead and back. The madman with bound hands was wriggling among them like an eel, spitting and kicking, while they were just roaring with laughter and poking him with the cigarettes over and over again.

"*Russe! Retten!** *Russe!*" the madman screamed desperately.

Ivan tensed—those bastards, what else were they doing there? Why were they so merciless and inhumane to both their own people and strangers, to everyone? Could they possibly be so low-minded and hungry for amusement?

They appeared to be waiting for something. But for what? Perhaps, for some help? One way or the other, there was little to fear now—that was the ultimate *finita,* as Giulia put it. His fourth time on the run would probably be the last. He only felt sorry for that little miracle, that long-legged black-eyed chatterbox. Their shared happiness had been so intoxicating and short-lived! Although, to be honest, he was still grateful to God, or, maybe, accident, for sending her his way at the very end. After all that had happened, it would still be easier to die with Giulia at his side than in the insatiable furnace of a crematorium.

Giulia seemed to have finished crying. Her sniffling stopped, her shoulders no longer shook but simply shivered from time to time, apparently from the cold. He took off the jacket, reached over to her and wrapped it gently around her body. Giulia started at his touch. She must have managed to pull herself together, for she sat up and began carefully rubbing her tear-stained eyes with her dirty, skinned little fists.

"Bad, *Ivanio*. Oh, oh, bad!"

"It's all right, it's all right. Don't be afraid! There're two cartridges here," he pointed to the pistol.

---

* *Retten!* – save! (German)

"*Non fortuna* Giulia. *Fine. Fine vita*[*] Giulia," she kept saying mournfully.

He was turning around on the ground, watching the Germans, and everything inside of him was writhing from helplessness and despair. He continued to feel morally responsible for her life—but what could be done? If only the cliff had been at least a little more accessible. Unfortunately, a ledge hung over the abyss, another one protruded below the overhang. Where the bottom was, no one could tell in the gloomy fog. Again, with his injured leg, how could he possibly keep his footing on that cliff?

"*Russe, retten! Russe!*" the madman was shouting from the saddle in a weakened voice.

Meanwhile, Giulia spotted the Germans on the mountain, rose to her knees and started shaking her little fists at them in a peevish, threatening manner.

"*Fascista! Briganti!* Bastards! *Nehmt uns doch!*[**] Come on!

The saddle grew quiet, but they soon heard a distant muffled voice carried by the wind.

"Hey, *Russ* and *Hure!* We you *kaputt* soon!"

It was followed by another voice, "*Komm* camp! Goodbye cold mountain. *Spazieren*[***] to hot *Krematorium.*"

Giulia's face lit up again with impetuous anger.

"*Herkommen!*" she shook her fists. "*Komm nehm ihr herkommen und uns holen! Nah, ihr Angst!*[****]"

---

[*]   *Fine vita* – end of life (Italian)

[**]   *Nehmt uns doch!* – take us then! (German)

[***]   *Spazieren* – walk (German)

[****]   *Komm nehm ihr herkommen und uns holen! Nah, ihr Angst!* - Come on! Come and get us! Aha, you're afraid! (German)

As the sound of her voice faded in the wind, the Germans began shouting obscenities, trying to outdo one another. Giulia was biting her lips, anguished by her helplessness in that duel. Seeing that, Ivan took her by the shoulders and held her close. She moved forward submissively, leaned on his chest and, like a little child, burst into tears, weeping quietly in inconsolable despair.

"Oh, don't. Don't. It's okay," he was lamely comforting her, trying with all his might to stifle emotion and despair.

Giulia seemed to calm down soon, and he held her in his embrace for a long time, thinking bleakly how well everything had begun and how inappropriately it was all about to end. He had to be an absolute loser, the most pathetic of all people—he had blown such an opportunity. Four lads had died to create it. Golodai, Yanushka and the others would probably have done far better—they would have already reached Trieste, joined the partisans and started killing the Krauts, but Ivan had got stuck in those damned mountains, and, to make matters worse, allowed himself to be driven into a trap like a wolf. Too bad, he should have done what he had set out to do and blown up that bomb, letting the savvier ones escape. And yet there he was. Moreover, he had destroyed Giulia, who had come to trust him. He had lived up to her hopes, he had indeed! That was doubly unfortunate and painful—all his efforts had proved futile, all his hopes had been dashed so ridiculously and haplessly.

He was holding her tear-stained face close to his chest and vaguely feeling her pain as well as the tenderness of her hands on his shoulders through his sufferings. Even now he found himself moved to the depth of his heart, and that made him feel even worse.

Giulia sat down beside him and adjusted her wind-scattered hair.

"Little, little hair. *Non* big hair. Never."

He was sitting opposite her and just gritting his teeth in despair. His mind simply could not come to terms with their inevitable death. But what could they do?

"*Ivanio!*" she suddenly exclaimed in an animated voice. "Let *mangiare Brot*. Eat bread!"

She took their crumbled ration out of her pocket and broke it in half with an unexpected joy in her sad eyes.

"Take, *Ivanio!*"

He took it. The piece was bigger than the one in her hand, but Ivan did not divide and compare now. That was no longer so important. With great and inexplicable pleasure, they swallowed the bread, all that was left of the supply he had been saving for the bear's ridge, and he felt the inevitability of the end with a new sadness. Oddly enough, that ration suddenly struck him as their last lifeline. By eating it they seemed to have turned the page on all the anxieties of their lives, and nothing was left except to wait for a few minutes and then get it over with. Once again, Ivan was overwhelmed by sorrow at the futility of his great efforts and their timing. The lads in the east had already liberated his homeland, reached the borders of the Soviet Union, but he would never make it home despite trying so hard to rejoin them.

Giulia was wringing her hands, despairingly examining the nooks and crannies of the gloomy, wild mountainous landscape and taking quick glances at the Germans, who were sitting and guarding them.

"*Ivanio!* Where *ist* God? Where *ist Madonna?* Where *ist* justice? Why *non* punish *fascismo?*" she asked again and again, stretching out her thin dark wrists on her knees.

"There is justice!" he shouted, roused by grief. "There will be punishment! There will!"

"Where *ist* punish? Where? English? *Americano? Unione Sovietica?*"

"Yes! The Soviet Union! If anyone, it won't forgive them! It'll break those bastards' backs!"

"Yes? Truth? *Unione Sovietica* strong? Truth?"

"Well, of course."

Giulia started towards him with a sudden hope in her eyes.

"It *gut?* Just? Noble? *Ivanio* tell *non* truth yesterday, yes? Joke, yes?"

Sensing the meaning of the words that had burst out of her sorrow-filled heart, Ivan stiffened as if someone had struck him. He thought hard for a few seconds and then saw Giulia, himself, his distant motherland, all it had been for him all his life and all it could be, in an entirely new light.

"Yes!" he said resolutely. "I was joking. I was lying. It was all false. My motherland is wonderful. Good. Just. There's none like it. No better people or land! And the best is yet to come! After the war! When Hitler is hanged. You'll see."

Yielding to an irresistible impulse, he ripped a handful of coarse mossy growth from the stones on the ground. A turbulent wave of unbearably sad feelings towards his distant country welled up in his heart, reaching his throat and choking him. He could no longer say anything. For the first time in his life he felt on the verge of tears.

Apparently noticing his struggle, Giulia touched his knee gently.

"Why say so joke? Bad joke."

"Sorry."

The Germans' puzzlement at their frivolity turned out to be brief. One of them soon grabbed an assault rifle and fired a burst without aiming. The bullets hit stones here and there, kicking up puffs of smoke, which were immediately caught by the wind. Ivan yanked Giulia by a flap of her jacket, and she reluctantly hunched and hid her head behind a stone. *Shoot, shoot, bastards! Let them hear,* he thought, remembering the camp inmates, who always listened to every shot in the mountains. *Let them know we're still alive!*

For several minutes, they lay behind the stone barrier and listened to the spring thunder of rumbling bursts over the ravine. However, bullets rarely reached them—the Germans seemed to be shooting to scare rather than kill. The assault rifles eventually went silent. The now remote, scattered echo had not yet faded when they heard new, very familiar sounds in the distance below the meadow. Throwing up her head, Giulia tried to say something but Ivan motioned her to keep quiet. Both of them pricked up their ears, looking intensely at each other, and then Ivan swore angrily—dogs were barking behind the saddle.

God knows what happened to him next as suppressed old rage suddenly exploded in his chest. Ivan started, rose heavily, planting his aching feet wide, and stood still—bent over, frightful, furious and oblivious to danger.

"Beasts!" he shouted at the Germans. "Jackals! Scared yourself and bringing in help? Come on, bring them over! Let them loose! Like hell you'll make it! Huh? You won't take us! Huh? Got it?"

It would probably have been easy for them to shoot him dead, but they did not shoot. Quiet now, the Germans were trying to make sense of the *Flugpunkt's* sudden rebellion, but they were hardly able to understand it. Apparently caused by agitation, a sudden chill shot through Ivan's body. He broke into shivers—fever seemed to be setting in. Having screamed his heart out, he was now instinctively looking around. The sky had become a little clearer, glittering blue gaps lit up by the morning sun had appeared in the cloudy veil. The bear's ridge they had failed to reach seemed about to sail into view from behind the clouds. Ivan longed to see the sun in the sky, but it was not there yet, and his heart sank.

He lowered himself to the ground, no longer interested in what was about to happen—he knew everything in advance. He did not even look at the dogs when they appeared in the saddle. Ivan felt their presence by the barking and commotion. The Alsatians must have followed their trail all the time and had probably gone berserk in the frenzy of pursuit.

Giulia suddenly threw herself towards him, bent over and shielded her face with her hands.

"Oh! *Non* dog! *Non* dog! *Ivanio, erschiessen! Erschiessen!*"

Having exploded within him, his rage and confusion immediately subsided. Ivan grew calm and steady again, with only one thought weighing on his mind—they had to get it over with. To kill himself was easy, but to take Giulia's life was far more difficult. And yet he had no other choice. He could not allow the SS men to goad them alive back to the camp and hang them to intimidate others—no, let them drag their dead bodies. If they had failed to gain freedom, they should at least cause trouble by their death.

At that moment, the Germans let the dogs loose.

One, two, three, four, five unleashed Alsatians shot downhill, stretching themselves out to full length as they ran. They were followed by the Germans. Immediately realising that they would attack in a few seconds, Ivan jumped to his feet and yanked Giulia by the hand, while she flung herself on his neck and burst into tears. Deep in his heart he felt that that he had to say something—the main, the most important words, but speech failed him for some reason. The dogs were already racing along the ravine. And so he wrenched her away and pushed her towards the edge of the cliff, towards the chasm. Giulia was not fighting, she was just sniffling like a suffocating person. Her eyes became huge, but there were no tears in them, only a suppressed mute fear and a stifled scream.

Standing on the edge, he glanced into the depth of the chasm—it was still gloomy, dank and cold. However, the fog inside it had thinned, and white snowy patches had become more visible. One of them climbed uphill like a long narrow tongue, and he suddenly felt a glimmer of hope—powerful, thrilling and frightening. Afraid that he would be too late, Ivan never said anything. Instead, he lowered the already raised pistol and pushed Giulia towards the very edge of the chasm.

"Jump!"

She immediately recoiled in fear. "Jump down to the snow!" he shouted again, but she shrank back with all her body and squeezed her eyes shut.

Meanwhile, loud barking erupted right behind their backs, and Ivan knew that the dogs had burst out onto the swell behind them. Clenching the pistol in his teeth, he jumped over to the girl. With sudden force, he grabbed her by the collar and trousers, swung her overhead and flung her wildly, sending her feet first into the precipice. At the last moment, he managed to notice her sprawled body flash over the ledge. Whether or not she had landed on the snow, he did not see. His only thought was that he would never manage such a jump with his bad leg.

The dogs went into a barking frenzy at the sight of him, and Ivan took two steps back to the chasm. A lean barrel-chested hound with only one ear sticking up on its head and the other one strangely missing was racing towards him in front of the pack. It leapt over the stones and flew to its hind legs right next to Ivan. Without aiming but with unhurried, almost inhuman attention, he fired into its gaping toothy mouth and then, unable to help it, at the next dog. The one-eared Alsatian flew and skidded past him into the chasm. Unfortunately, the other one was not alone. Two more dogs were running beside it, and Ivan wondered for a split-second whether or not he had hit the target.

His uncertainty was cut short by a ferocious blow to the chest. Unbearable pain pierced his throat, he caught a glimpse of the cloudy sky, and everything went numb forever.

In lieu of an Epilogue

"Greetings to Ivan's family, greetings to the people who knew him, greetings to the village of Tsyareshki near the Two Blue Lakes in Belarus.

Writing to you is Giulia Novelli from Rome. Please do not be surprised that an unfamiliar signora knows your Ivan, knows Tsyareshki near the Two Blue Lakes in Belarus.

Of course, you have not forgotten that dreadful time for Europe—the dark night of humanity that saw thousands of people die, often in despair. While losing their lives, some accepted death as a blessed release from the torments of Nazism. That gave them strength to meet their end in a worthy manner and not violate their conscience. Others brought death to her knees in a heroic struggle. They left a high example of courage to humanity and died, surprising even their enemies, who did not feel satisfied with their victory, so relative was their triumph.

Among those people was your compatriot Ivan Tsyareshka, who met me by the will of providence on the difficult paths of unequal struggle and losses. I was privileged to share in the last three days of his life—three days of love, learning and happiness, huge as eternity itself. However, it was not God's will for me to also share in his death; fate—or an ordinary unmelted snowdrift—prevented me from dying in a chasm that I would have preferred to a crematorium. Afterwards I was picked up by a person who was not without a kind heart. Of course, that happened later, but at that first moment in the chasm, the minute I opened my eyes and realised that I was alive, Ivan was no longer among the living. The wailing of the dogs was dying down under the clouds, and the echo of the last two shots was still rumbling through the ravine.

Gradually I came back to life, which at first seemed totally meaningless without him. All I had during the long months of loneliness were the three tragic and happy days lived with him. I could describe what kind of person he was, but I think that you know him better than I do. I would only like to say that all my subsequent life has been illuminated by the bright light of my meeting with this man, and so have my modest civil society work at the Union for Peace, my service on the editorial board of a trade union newspaper, and, finally, my efforts to bring up my son Giovanni, who is already eighteen years old and studying to be a journalist. (By the way, he is the one who translated this letter into Russian. Although I have also learnt the language, my Russian is certainly not as perfect as his.) In my study I have a map of Belarus, the country Ivan loved so dearly. Unfortunately, I cannot find the village of Tsyareshki near the Two Lakes on it. I hope that you will generously help me. And one more thing—a photo. I would like to have a photo of Ivan, however poor, as a child, as a young man, or, better still, as a soldier.

While remembering him, I sometimes shudder to think that I could have ended up in a different camp or never seen his fight with the *Kommandoführer* and run after him following that memorable explosion, that I could have passed by him in life, coming close but never making contact. But that did not happen, and now I thank providence for all the trials that fell to my lot, all the laws and coincidences that brought us together with him and changed my whole life so unexpectedly.

That is all. *Finito.*

Farewell, his unknown compatriots, farewell, his family, farewell, the distant Tsyareshki near the Two Blue Lakes. I also longed to live near them. Do not forget your countryman as we do not forget him.

With gratitude to all those who bore, raised and knew this man, truly Russian in his kindness and worthy of admiration in his courage.

Thank you, thank you for everything.

With respect and love for you,

Giulia Novelli in Rome."

Dear Reader,

Thank you for purchasing this book.

We at Glagoslav Publications are glad to welcome you, and hope that you find our books to be a source of knowledge and inspiration.

We want to show the beauty and depth of the Slavic region to everyone looking to expand their horizon and learn something new about different cultures, different people, and we believe that with this book we have managed to do just that.

Now that you've got to know us, we want to get to know you. We value communication with our readers and want to hear from you! We offer several options:

– Join our Book Club on Goodreads, Library Thing and Shelfari, and receive special offers and information about our giveaways;

– Share your opinion about our books on Amazon, Barnes & Noble, Waterstones and other bookstores;

– Join us on Facebook and Twitter for updates on our publications and news about our authors;

– Visit our site www.glagoslav.com to check out our Catalogue and subscribe to our Newsletter.

Glagoslav Publications is getting ready to release a new collection and planning some interesting surprises — stay with us to find out!

Glagoslav Publications
Office 36, 88-90 Hatton Garden
EC1N 8PN London, UK
Tel: + 44 (0) 20 32 86 99 82
Email: contact@glagoslav.com

Leo Tolstoy – Flight from Paradise

by Pavel Basinsky

Over a hundred years ago, something truly outrageous occurred at Yasnaya Polyana. Count Leo Tolstoy, a famous author aged eighty-two at the time, took off, destination unknown. Since then, the circumstances surrounding the writer's whereabouts during his final days and his eventual death have given rise to many myths and legends. In this book, popular Russian writer and reporter Pavel Basinsky delves into the archives and presents his interpretation of the situation prior to Leo Tolstoy's mysterious disappearance. Basinsky follows Leo Tolstoy throughout his life, right up to his final moments. Reconstructing the story from historical documents, he creates a visionary account of the events that led to the Tolstoys' family drama.

Flight from Paradise will be of particular interest to international researchers studying Leo Tolstoy's life and works, and is highly recommended to a broader audience worldwide.

Buy it > www.glagoslav.com

The Investigator

by Margarita Khemlin

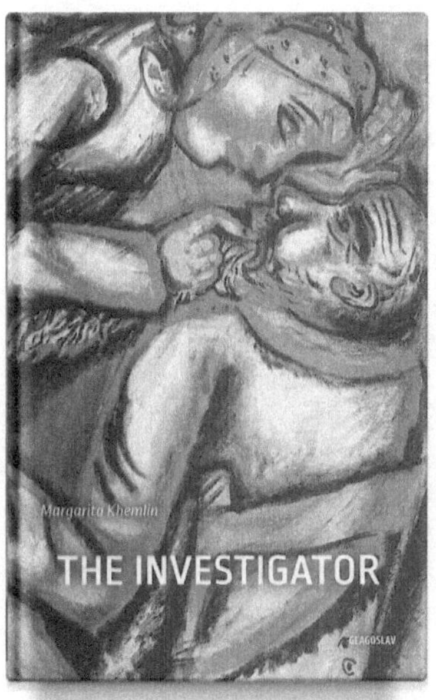

The Investigator is set in Soviet Ukraine in the early 1950s. With Stalin at the helm, the post-war Soviet Union is struggling to rebuild and to heal the nation of its multiple wounds. Plots and conspiracies abound and challenges to socialist values, real and imagined, proliferate.

A young woman is murdered in a typical Soviet town. In the spirit of the era everyone is a suspect. The investigator of the title sets out to solve the crime. A former intelligence officer who seeks to embody the ideals of the young Soviet Union, he introduces the reader to a polyphony of alternative voices that, together with his own, weave the unique fabric of this striking novel.

Buy it > www.glagoslav.com

Glagoslav Publications Catalogue

- *The Time of Women* by Elena Chizhova
- *Sin* by Zakhar Prilepin
- *Hardly Ever Otherwise* by Maria Matios
- *Khatyn* by Ales Adamovich
- *Christened with Crosses* by Eduard Kochergin
- *The Vital Needs of the Dead* by Igor Sakhnovsky
- *A Poet and Bin Laden* by Hamid Ismailov
- *Kobzar* by Taras Shevchenko
- *White Shanghai* by Elvira Baryakina
- *The Stone Bridge* by Alexander Terekhov
- *King Stakh's Wild Hunt* by Uladzimir Karatkevich
- *Depeche Mode* by Serhii Zhadan
- *Herstories*, An Anthology of New Ukrainian Women Prose Writers
- *The Battle of the Sexes Russian Style* by Nadezhda Ptushkina
- *A Book Without Photographs* by Sergey Shargunov
- *Sankya* by Zakhar Prilepin
- *Wolf Messing - The True Story of Russia`s Greatest Psychic*
  by Tatiana Lungin
- *Good Stalin* by Victor Erofeyev
- *Solar Plexus* by Rustam Ibragimbekov
- *Don't Call me a Victim!* by Dina Yafasova
- *A History of Belarus* by Lubov Bazan
- *Children's Fashion of the Russian Empire* by Alexander Vasiliev
- *Empire of Corruption - The Russian National Pastime*
  by Vladimir Soloviev
- *Heroes of the 90s - People and Money. The Modern History of Russian Capitalism*
- *Boris Yeltsin - The Decade that Shook the World* by Boris Minaev
- *A Man Of Change - A study of the political life of Boris Yeltsin*
- *Gnedich* by Maria Rybakova
- *Marina Tsvetaeva - The Essential Poetry*
- *Multiple Personalities* by Tatyana Shcherbina
- *The Investigator* by Margarita Khemlin
- *Leo Tolstoy – Flight from paradise* by Pavel Basinsky
- *Moscow in the 1930s* by Natalia Gromova
- *Prisoner* by Anna Nemzer

More coming soon...